MW00959068

IRONBORN:
PROJECT 1711

By: Kyler Wright

This book is dedicated to
my mom, the original influencer of my
writing dream.

TABLE OF CONTENTS

Prologue

Starport Ave, Union
New Jersey, USA
9:30 p.m.
Jordan

Jordan ran down the road, looking from side to side, trying to find an escape. A bulky, armored black van sped down the road, chasing after him at nearly seventy miles an hour. Jordan, however, was faster.

He quickly turned down an alley on his left, stumbling slightly in the process but ultimately managing to keep his balance. He looked over his shoulder, disappointed to find that the van was just small enough to fit down the alley, its sides brushing against the red brick walls. From Jordan's perspective, the van moved sluggishly, slowing down as he sped up. As the van fell behind his inhuman speed, there was only one thing that Jordan truly had to worry about:

Bullets.

The windows of the van rolled down and Jordan felt pieces of shrapnel dig into his shoulder. He winced as the gunfire from gang members inside the vehicle missed the quickly moving boy and hit the brick wall beside him. Using his powerful legs, Jordan quickly jumped up on top of the wall, making it effectively impossible for half of the van's occupants to hit him.

The windows to the apartments in the building beside him sped by every few seconds, his muscular, dark-skinned figure flashing into view for a brief moment each time before disappearing again. Formulating a plan in his mind, he ran along the thin strip of brick before he located the next window to his left and dove through.

The previously sleeping apartment was now filled with the noise of shattering glass and flying bullets as the occupants of the van continued to fire at Jordan until he passed out of view.

As he ran through the small apartment and out into the hallway, Jordan heard the whirring and slam of the van's doors. He ran down the open air concrete passage, doors blurring by him until he reached the end. In front of him was a staircase and beyond that, a two story drop to the ground.

Hearing a noise, Jordan turned in surprise to find one of his enemies facing him from down the hallway, using a hand-held machine gun to rip bullets down the hall. Jordan barely managed to make it around the corner of a wall without getting hit. He pulled out a simple handgun from his hip in case he came across another opponent but kept running, not daring to face an enemy with such firepower.

As he neared a flight of concrete stairs, a second enemy appeared from around a corner in front of him. Being this close, Jordan could now see that these were no ordinary gang members like ones that he had been hunted by in the past. They, like their van, were plated with shiny black armor and helmets, looking more like something from the future than a gang member from the streets.

With his gun already drawn, Jordan shot his pistol, but the bullet simply hit the soldier's armor, causing no harm. Caught off guard by the enemy's immunity, he was not quick enough to escape as the soldier grabbed his arm and took a swing at his head.

Jordan dodged out of the way, again startled as the soldier's fist went a few inches into the concrete wall behind him, even though he seemed to feel no pain.

Thinking quickly, Jordan rammed his shoulder into the soldier's chest, throwing them both off balance and sending them tumbling down the stairs.

Their descent stopped as the stairs turned sharply, and Jordan felt his head slam into a metal railing. As he struggled to stand, the soldier again grabbed him, but this time Jordan managed to get an upper hand, pushing the soldier and knocking both of them over the stairway railing down to the ground below. After quickly brushing off the pain of the landing, Jordan grabbed the soldier's much more powerful gun and fired it into their head.

To his surprise, the soldier's head exploded with a shower of sparks, sending small metal fragments across the grass as Jordan shielded his eyes. Where the soldier's head had met his neck was now a mesh of exposed wires. Jordan blinked in disbelief as he suddenly noticed the rest of the body in closer detail. The light aluminum skeleton, the dragon steel fiber armor, everything being welded together and interlaced with wires. This was no gang member or even a human soldier, this was a robot.

Jordan heard loud mechanical footsteps from somewhere inside the building. He tried to grab the robot's gun but found that it was attached to the soldier's body by a cord, so he dropped it and continued running.

Another soldier came into view as it turned into the parking lot of the apartment building on a shiny black motorcycle. Jordan ran straight at it, catching the soldier off guard with his blinding speed.

Jordan dodged the bike at the last second and hit the driver with the back of his gun, throwing the new soldier onto the pavement. In the same motion, Jordan grabbed the bike, hopped on and sped out of the parking lot down the deserted road.

"To Cadmore Industries" He assured himself under his breath, "To safety."

Jordan had only been on the bike for a few seconds before he heard a gunshot and could feel small chips of pavement dig into the back of his legs. He turned around and his vision focused, seeming to zoom in on a sniper positioned on the roof of the apartment building, who was pulling back the bolt on his gun to reload. Jordan half-blindly fired backward, missing every time.

As he turned forwards again, he was startled to see

a second black van blocking the road directly in front of him. He tried to move out of the way but lost control and slammed into the side of the van. Jordan tumbled down onto the asphalt and felt a stab of pain as his fall tore a large gash in his side. As Jordan lost his focus, time returned to normal. Before he could get up however, he was surrounded by a ring of robots as they poured out of the barely dented van.

A human officer stepped forward through the ring of towering figures. "I see that you are the first to experience the power of our new infantry, the Enforcement from Cadmore Industries." He sneered. "The tides have turned for your kind."

Jordan tried desperately to rise back up but was quickly beaten back to the ground as a metal foot slammed into his wounded side, cracking multiple ribs.

"As you know," The officer continued seamlessly, "These new soldiers are especially fortified. Even so, they took a while to capture you. Your blood is very strong."

"If you live in my house, being strong is a way of survival," Jordan spat. "If I wasn't strong then I wouldn't be here."

The officer smiled. "Strong but arrogant. Vrazda will not take someone like this. Get rid of him." He motioned his hand to the soldiers surrounding the boy, and one raised its gun towards Jordan's already bleeding body.

The last thing Jordan saw were two words inscribed

in silver on the side of the robot's gun. Those two words were ones that would have once given him hope. A sense of friendship. A sense of safety. The place that was once a haven was now a prison. Jordan read the words slowly, and they rang out in his mind as a bullet pierced his heart.

Cadmore Industries

Jordan had done nothing wrong. He had committed no crimes. He had never even met his assailants. All he had done was be born different.

And now he was dead.

PART I

A WARRIOR'S BEGINNINGS

1- An Act Of Bravery

Torman High School, Sacramento
California, U.S.A
2:15 p.m.
Flynn

Flynn slid four quarters across the counter to the cashier, picked up his drink and walked out the door beside his two friends. With the final day of ninth grade behind them, they had decided to finish the year off with their daily tradition of walking up to the gas station to buy Julios.

Flynn popped the lid off of the glass bottle in his hand, taking a refreshing sip. There was nothing quite like fizzy fruit juice on a hot summer day like this.

"I'm so glad I can put that year behind me," Jackson said from Flynn's right as the three friends walked down the road. "Summer might only be a few months, but at least it isn't that place." He inclined his head toward where they had been a few minutes ago. "Torman High School. Even the name sounds horrific."

"Tell me about it," Dominic said from Flynn's left. "If I had it my way, this summer would just last forever and we would never have to see that place again."

"Come on guys," Flynn said. "School isn't that bad."

"Are you kidding me?" Jackson looked at him through his messy blonde hair. "You're crazy, mate."

"I'm just saying," Flynn replied. "It could be worse." He knew that very well. Much more than either of his two friends.

"Like what?" Jackson asked. "I bet even people in military school would be scared to go to that place."

"I highly doubt that," Flynn said, taking another sip of his drink. Unlike Jackson and Dominic, Flynn knew what it was like to enjoy going to school. Not because it was fun, but because it was better than what awaited him when he wasn't there.

"I know why he enjoys school so much," Dominic said, a hint of mocking in his voice.

"Why is that, Dom?" Jackson asked.

"I think there might be a specific person that would make school slightly more..." Dominic spoke as if he was an investigator, rubbing his chin in thought. "Enticing."

Jackson smiled, understanding the joke. "A *very* specific person."

"You two are hilarious," Flynn said sarcastically, sipping his drink.

"Thanks," Jackson replied, smiling stupidly.

"We know you talked to her today," Dominic said, staring at Flynn intently.

Flynn looked over at him. Dom's one visible eye that wasn't covered by his dreads seemed to be boring into him, its hazelnut color contrasting his dark Jamaican skin.

"I don't even know who you're talking about," Flynn replied.

"Don't give me that," Jackson said before turning to Dom, changing his voice from its natural Australian accent to a french one, like someone from a movie. "Look at the glint in his eye. He is a man in love."

"He wants nothing more than to go back to that horrid place just so he can see her again," Dom said, going along with Jackson's melodramatic teasing. "To just get a glimpse of her, he would go through even the worst torture known to man. Homework."

Flynn just chuckled, looking at his two friends as their story grew.

"But then summer came along, breaking the two lovers apart for two weeks," Jackson said, placing his hands over his heart.

"It's three months," Dominic said, ending the act.

Jackson sniffed. "It feels like two weeks."

"So Flynn," Dominic shifted so he was shoulder-to-shoulder with his friend. "What did you do today?"

"I went to school," Flynn said nonchalantly. "Then I went to the gas station-"

"We mean with Emily," Jackson said, leaning in like Domonic had.

Flynn looked at the two of them. "I feel like I'm being interrogated here."

"Who says you aren't?" Jackson asked jokingly.

"You were five minutes late to our meeting place today," Dominic observed. "And for anyone who knows Flynn, they know that he's never late."

"Alright, alright," Flynn finally admitted. "I wanted to talk to her again before the school year ended so I found her before coming over to you guys."

"And?" Jackson urged him on.

Flynn shook his head, still not understanding why it was so important. "We wished each other a good summer, she gave me a hug, and then I left."

"A hug?" Jackson exclaimed.

"Here we go again," Flynn muttered.

Dom looked over at Jackson. "This is a huge step in the story line!"

"Guys," Flynn said. "It's a hug. That really isn't that big of a deal. You guys are acting like we're in second grade. We're just friends."

"Sure you are," Dom mocked.

"You are so stuck, man," Jackson laughed.

Flynn looked at him curiously. "Stuck?"

"On *her*," Jackson said, still chuckling.

Flynn raised an eyebrow. "I don't know what you're talking about." He continued walking, a smile on his face.

"Hey, at least Flynn talks to Emily," Dom said as he and Jackson followed him down the sidewalk. "I don't see you ever talking to Haley."

"That's an entirely different situation," Jackson countered.

"Oh yeah?" Flynn asked. "In what way?"

"Haley is on a new level, mate," he responded.

"Whatever you say," Dom said. "Besides, Cago is the real one who needs help. His self-esteem around girls is horrific. Or around anyone for that matter."

"Speaking of which," Flynn said, "Where is Cago?" Cago was the shortest and quietest of the four friends. He had a pale, Asian complexion, and dark black hair that was always uncombed and constantly falling into his eyes. He normally walked home with the rest of them, but he hadn't shown up today.

"Not sure," Jackson said.

Flynn had noticed the disappearance of their fourth friend earlier in the day. To most people it wouldn't seem like a big deal but to Flynn it made him nervous. He knew who Cago might be, and knew what him not being here could mean.

As the three friends turned a corner on the sidewalk, a large, matte black military vehicle lumbered past them. It had six tires and rose high above any other vehicles it drove next to, as if asserting its dominance as it broadcasted two letters, which were painted in blue on the side of the vehicle. C.I.

"An Enforcement transport," Dominic whistled. "Not every day that you see one of those."

Flynn tensed. That phrase was true for most people, but for Flynn, he praised the days where he never had to see one.

"Have you guys heard of the new announcement that Cadmore Industries made last week?" Jackson asked as the vehicle's rumbling disappeared into the distance.

"No," Dom responded casually.

"The Industry is starting a new development," Jackson sipped his drink. "Some kind of vehicle called a Raptor."

The Raptor Project. Flynn knew that the Ironborn Protection Agency had known about this project long before now. He could name every part and weak spot on one. But here with his friends, that wasn't who he was. He had to convince them that he had no idea what they were talking about, and make them believe it.

"Well it sounds pretty powerful," Jackson said. "Has some kind of rapid fire gun that can shred through enemy troops like nothing."

Flynn almost objected to this with the fact that Clan Xion's suits were now modified to be powerful enough that the troops could handle it, but luckily he caught himself just in time. "Sounds interesting," he said, taking another sip of his soda.

They walked in silence for a while, watching cars pass as they strolled down the sidewalk through the neighborhoods.

Jackson raised his glass into the air. "To Flynn!" he called. "And for his act of bravery!"

"My act of bravery?" Flynn asked, bewildered.

"You finally got a hug from Emily!" Jackson explained.

"To Flynn!" Dom agreed.

"Well you don't have to shout what I've done to the whole world," Flynn said quietly.

"Well, I haven't told them what you did yet," Jackson said. He raised his glass again. "To Flynn! For almost getting kissed by a not-so-hot girl!" He smiled and turned to Flynn. "Now I have."

"Alright, first of all, we just hugged. And second-"

"Yeah yeah, whatever," Jackson mumbled. "No need to be so analytical."

"I just don't think it's that big of a deal," Flynn said. If only they knew how big of a deal it really was to him.

"Of course it isn't a big deal," Dom said. "But we still like to make fun of you for it." They all chuckled.

Jackson took another sip of his drink. "You know,

we're just like an Enforcement squad."

Flynn twitched. "What do you mean?"

Jackson was a little confused by Flynn's reaction but brushed it off. "I mean we've got all the people, you know? Dom's the athletic one, Flynn's the analytical one, Cago's the sneaky one, and I'm the strong one."

Dom laughed. "You're not the strong one."

"Sure I am!" Jackson motioned toward himself. "Have you even seen all this?"

"Yes, many times," Dom said. "And I'd still say Flynn has you beat."

"No way," Jackson scoffed. He turned to Flynn. "What do you think?"

Flynn shrugged. "How would I know?"

"I think Flynn would be the humble one," Dom said with a chuckle. "He'd win in a fight against you any day."

"Like today?" Jackson said, raising an eyebrow.

"Normally I'd accept," Flynn said. "But I wouldn't want to hurt you at the beginning of the summer. It would ruin your whole 'two week' vacation."

Dom laughed. "Maybe not quite the most humble one."

As the friends rounded the next corner, Flynn realized they were nearly at the end of their route. Or, at least, where Flynn would split apart from them. Dominic and Jackson lived in the same neighborhood, which was only about half a mile past Flynn's.

"Do you want to come with me and Jackson to hang out at my house?" Dominic asked.

Flynn shook his head. "I wish I could. My parents want me home."

"Your parents?" Jackson asked. "They don't come home from work for hours!"

"Still, I want to follow the rules," Flynn said.

"Flynn has always been a saint," Dom said, chuckling. "I bet my mom would trade me for you if she could."

"I think she'd trade you for anyone," Jackson mocked.

"Other than you," Dom countered.

Jackson made a face at him.

The group paused as the sidewalk turned.

"The infamous road," Dom sighed, turning to Flynn. "Farewell my friend. It has been an honor serving beside you."

"Serving beside me?" Flynn asked with a chuckle. "Sometimes I wonder how I've stayed sane being friends with you two."

Jackson outstretched his hand, leading Flynn into a very complex handshake that they had perfected after a year of doing it every day. "I'm not sure you still are, mate."

"Well," Flynn sighed. "Hopefully we can hang out this summer."

"If not, I'll kidnap you," Jackson promised.

Flynn gave a confused smile. "That's very reassuring."

As the group split up, Flynn turned to go toward his house as his friends disappeared from sight. As soon as they did, Flynn suddenly changed direction, turning back up the road they had just traveled down. He hated lying to his friends but there were more important things. The less they knew about him the better.

Flynn walked up two blocks before turning left, sneaking down a small alleyway. In this part of Sacramento, the buildings were much older than the main city, and his house was one of the oldest.

Most people wouldn't even know it was a house, as everyone knew it as a bakery that had been allegedly abandoned for years, but that was perfect for Flynn.

Walking to the end of the alley, Flynn located the ladder that he used to get inside. He began to climb, mindlessly grabbing the rusted rungs that were bolted to the back of the red brick building. He made it up next to a second-story window, pulling it open and slipping inside.

Flynn set his backpack on the ground and sat on the end of his bland bed. Other than the few pieces of furniture, the room was empty, adding to the illusion that no one had been here for years. Despite this being his room, the bakery had never felt like home. This place hadn't been his true home for years.

Flynn walked over to the empty dresser, on which was a single picture of his parents. "Hey mom," he said, looking at them. "Dad," he sighed. "I talked to Emily again today. Jackson and Dominic gave me lots of trouble for it too," he chuckled. "Today was the last day of ninth grade. It's weird to look back and think that it's been three years..." He trailed off, looking at his reflection in the glass that covered their picture. He had his father's hair, wavy and dark, but his mother's bright hazel eyes. At least that's what people had told him years ago, back when people had known who his parents were. Who he was.

A noise pulled Flynn away from his thoughts. He turned to see that his cell phone, which he had thrown on his bed, was ringing. He picked it up, looking at the name of the caller. Instead of a name, there was just a dash. Flynn's eyes narrowed. He knew what this meant.

Flynn answered the call.

"Scorpius," the voice on the other side was toneless and muffled. "We have a positive report on Project 1697. Enforcement is moving in quickly."

Flynn exited his room, walking down the stairs into the bakery section of the building. "Do we have anyone on site?"

"Blackeye and the big man are already ready to intercept, and the sergeant is going to bring him to safety," the voice said. "We were sent here to get you."

Flynn opened the front door of the bakery, striding quickly down to the car that sat at the curb. To any regular person, it would seem to be a regular luxury SUV, but Flynn knew that unlike the car it was modeled after, this vehicle could take a considerably larger beating.

After hearing the click of the doors unlocking, Flynn pocketed his phone and opened the back door, hopping inside.

Because of security reasons, the voice had been altered on the phone call, making it so Flynn could not tell who was on the other side. As he looked at the driver, he was now able to tell who it had been.

"Zane?" Flynn asked. "You're not even old enough to drive!"

Zane turned to look back at Flynn, adjusting his neatly-combed blonde hair. "Well everyone who is old enough is already occupied. Besides, what is Enforcement going to do, arrest me?"

An identical face to Zane's poked out from the passenger seat. Ryan looked nearly the same as his twin brother but was much more carefree, with long, messy hair. "I tried to convince the sergeant to let me drive but she said I was 'too reckless' and gave the keys to Zane."

"That I can agree with," Flynn said as they pulled away from the bakery. "Where's our target?"

"Lendon Cemetery," Zane said, his eyes on the road. "Came up on our scanners a few minutes ago."

"Do you guys have my equipment?" Flynn asked.

"We grabbed them from the warehouse," Ryan replied. "They're in the back."

Flynn smiled. The warehouse. That was his true home.

Looking over the back of his seat, Flynn grabbed his four items. The first, his weapon of choice, a hiveblade. The second, a disk shaped shield-helmet, his mataka. The third, his sidearm, a gun that shot in quick and powerful bursts.

And the fourth, possibly most impressive of all, a small black box, that sat in a compartment on a slim black utility belt. To any regular person it might seem insignificant but Flynn knew how many times it had saved his life. It held his suit, which was identical to the ones that the other six members of his squad wore.

Attaching the belt around his waist, Flynn looked back up at Zane. "How far is it?"

"Only a few miles," Zane replied. "Are you feeling ready?"

"You know it," Flynn replied. Project 1697 was something Flynn had been working on for a long time now, and he wasn't about to let Cadmore Industries take it away from him.

2- Project 1697

Lendon Cemetery, Sacramento
California, USA
5:30 p.m.
Cago

Cago knelt on the ground, his wrinkled black suit brushing the damp grass. The overcast sky seemed to reflect his mood, dull and gray. Earlier rain had begun to pour, but that had passed and still Cago remained, hours after the others had left. He looked up at the mound of dirt in front of him, his eyes lingering on the flowers gently resting on top.

He had not cried. After all that had happened, he was not sure that he still could. His aunt was gone. Just like his brother. Just like his mom. Cago thought he could finally live happily without one of his family members dying, but that hope was gone now. There was nothing left for him here. Just cold, empty space.

Cago heard footsteps behind him. He caught a glimpse of a person approaching behind him on a reflective gravestone to his left. The figure was wearing a skin-tight dark gray suit that was highlighted with glowing red lines that traced up their body and was fitted with weapons and gadgets, a streamlined motorbike-like helmet concealing their face.

The figure leaned down and whispered in his ear, "You are no longer safe. They are moving in as we speak."

Cago wiped his nose with his sleeve and sniffed, "How much time do we have?"

"About fifteen minutes," The figure said. "But we need to be as cautious as possible."

Cago stood up slowly and turned toward the stranger, "I've heard of you guys before." He said. "You are part of the Ironborn Protection Agency, aren't you?"

The figure nodded and began leading him across the cemetery toward a small, sleek-looking car.

"Is that a Corvette?" He asked, surprised.

"A Lamborghini Huracán." She said, "Or an identical copy of one, that is." They reached the car and the figure got in. Cago hesitated. It was such a nice vehicle.

"Don't worry about scratching the car," the figure said. "It's bulletproof. Built by Clan Xion, like the rest of our cars and gear." Cago wasn't sure what Clan Xion was but he got in anyway, though still hesitantly.

The figure pressed a button on a black utility belt around their waist and Cago watched with wide eyes as the entire suit folded down into a tiny little box, the helmet seeming to magically fold down into the collar and the rest collapsing in from there. Even Cadmore Industries didn't have that type of technology. He had seen suits on IPA soldiers stop ammunition from tanks, but he had never thought that a suit with such strength could collapse into that small of a space. It was unbelievable.

"My name is Talia, but as a member of our organization you will call me Bi." She reached her hand across the middle console as she drove, and he shook it. She looked to be in her late twenties, with dark brown skin and black hair put up in an afro. Her brown eyes looked calm, but they had a penetrating, calculating feel to them, as if she observed everything. Every action. Every movement.

"You seem startled by our technology." She said, "If you're surprised now, you might want to be prepared for a lot more amazement in the near future."

"Where am I going?" He asked.

She smiled kindly. "As of right now, Mr. Z has selected you to be in Clan Dax. Although, based on my experiences with Captain Dax in the past, my guess is that you will be put in my squad. Dax prefers his soldiers to be a bit more..." She glanced over at the scrawny boy in the seat beside her, "muscular."

A voice came onto the radio, speaking quickly. "Bi, you need to turn around. They are waiting at the end of the road you are currently-"

Cago watched as they turned around a corner in the road, and his eyes grew wide as an intersection came into view. The intersection was a war zone. He saw Enforcement robots battling against a half-dozen IPA soldiers, each wearing suits with blood red highlights, just like Bi's. Two of them stood back to back, fighting in near unison. Another was taller than most of the surrounding buildings, and was using four arms to pulverize the enemy.

Bi grabbed a lever to her right and turned the steering wheel, drifting the car in a tight circle. "That manual hand brake was added in by Zane," Bi said, her voice far too calm for their current situation. "It helps for quick maneuvering."

"Zane?" Cago asked, his voice unsteady as he gripped the armrests of his seat.

"One of my soldiers," Bi said. "You might meet him someday." She looked behind them to see that four armored truck-like Enforcement vehicles had followed them out of the intersection, and were beginning to fire at them with the turrets that were mounted in the back.

Out of instinct, Cago ducked, and a dark mist surrounded the area around the car like octopus ink. The Enforcement bots, now unable to see, ran into the barrier on the side of the road as they rounded a corner before rolling and disappearing from sight.

Bi looked over at him. "Was that one of your powers?"

He nodded, still a little shaken from the danger they had just escaped.

"Good move," she said in approval. "You'll make a fine soldier."

"Are they getting in the car?" Flynn asked.

Blackeye, who was looking through the scope of her sniper rifle, looked up at Flynn and nodded. Flynn had been set up with Blackeye as a scouting post, reporting back to Squad Sergeant Bi with any signs of Enforcement moving in. Blackeye didn't speak to anyone except for the sergeant. No one knew why, she just didn't. Flynn had mostly gotten used to it, but it was still a little unnerving at times.

"Let's get to the next post," Flynn said, walking down the small hill they were currently on. Blackeye followed behind after folding up the tripod on her sniper rifle and slinging it over her shoulder.

Flynn had been the one put in charge of studying Project 1697. The boy, Cago, had been one of Flynn's friends for a while, and it wasn't until recently that he had begun to notice small signs that he might be one of them. It was a good thing they had been watching over him since then, otherwise Enforcement might have caught him first.

Flynn pressed a button on his wrist, turning on his comm link. "This is Scorpius, we are at the second post."

"Affirmative." He heard Ryan's voice come through the speakers in his helmet. He was breathing heavily, as if he had just run a marathon.

Flynn and Blackeye began to hear noises as they made their way toward the next ridge. The battle had begun. They started running.

When they got to the top of the next hill, they overlooked mayhem. At an intersection between two roads, Tarff, Ryan, and Zane battled against a platoon of Enforcement robots.

Tarff, at nearly twenty feet tall, towered over the enemies, throwing them and their vehicles all over the place with his four arms. Zane and Ryan fought back to back with both gun and sword, also commanding a dozen of their own robots to fight for them, which they themselves had built.

Flynn turned to Blackeye. "Cover me. I'm going in."

She nodded, dropped to a kneeling position and began firing down at the enemy soldiers.

Flynn drew his hiveblade and charged down the hill into the battle. He had used the same weapons all three years he had been in this war. His hiveblade, and his mataka. The hiveblade was shaped like a staff, but had a blade protruding from each end. The mataka was a shield-like helmet that he could use for blocking attacks, or throwing at enemies. Both of the items were antiques from an ancient Chinese war that he had gotten from his grandfather, who was an archeologist. After joining the IPA, Zane had reinforced them with the IPA's dragon steel, making them strong enough to even stop bullets.

Flynn stabbed the nearest robot through the chest with his Hiveblade, using his momentum to drive it into the ground as other robots turned to confront him.

Without his suit or his powers, Flynn would be dead right now. The suits, like most of the IPA's technology, were designed by Clan Xion. They were durable enough to stop bullets by the hundreds, as well as giving you strength to be able to move quicker, run faster, and lift more weight.

And then of course, there was Flynn's big secret: his powers.

Flynn was part of a super human race called the Ironborn. Because of many past events, the Ironborn had been labeled as evil, and most of them had been killed off. Flynn and the rest of the surviving Ironborn were now either in hiding or helping the Ironborn Protection Agency, the IPA, fight back against their enemies, like Enforcement, while also trying to find the other remaining Ironborn and bring them to safety.

Cago, or Project 1697, was an Ironborn. Flynn had studied him for a while now, trying to see if he had powers. Apparently, at the death of his aunt, some part of his powers had manifested themselves enough for some kind of radiation to show up on one of Zane's scanners and now they were here to bring him to safety before Cadmore Industries killed him. Luckily, the Ironborn were difficult to kill.

Difficult, but far from impossible.

Flynn reached out with his powers and sent a robot flying into his comrade, throwing them both to the ground. He then pulled his mataka off of his head mount where it was currently sitting as a helmet and threw the disk through a group of soldiers, using his powers to propel the weapon at an extremely high speed before using his abilities again to summon the shield back to him, where he attached it to the mount on his arm. He charged forward, cutting through enemies with his blade and bashing robots aside with his shield. An Enforcement army vehicle swerved in front of him, blocking his way.

Moving quickly, Flynn put his shield back onto his head mount and jumped over the vehicle in a spinning side-flip-like manner, keeping the top of his head constantly aimed at the vehicle so that the bullets coming from the soldiers inside would hit his shield instead of him. While in the air, he dropped one of the small, round explosives from his belt, and the vehicle was obliterated behind him as he landed on the other side.

Flynn ran to where his comrades were fighting. Looking up one of the roads that came to the intersection, Flynn saw the Lamborghini heading straight for the battle.

"Bi," he said into his helmet's built-in comm. "You need to turn around. They are waiting at the end of the road you are currently-"

It was too late. The car had already turned into the view of the intersection.

When Bi saw the battle taking place, she quickly swerved sideways, drifting into a full one-eighty degree turn and speeding away from the battle. A few robot cars chased them in pursuit, and they disappeared around the corner.

Flynn continued fighting beside his teammates. He stabbed and bashed and shot until the robots began to diminish. It took about ten minutes before Blackeye took out the last soldier, and it collapsed to the ground with a hole through its head.

"That was quite a skirmish," Tarff said as he shrunk down to his normal size of six-foot four, his two extra arms shrinking into his body and disappearing.

"Well, it was worth it," They all heard Bi say through their comms. "The project is safe."

3-Meetings

Clan Vilo Meeting Office
Classified Location
7:30 p.m.
Talia

Talia walked down the dim office hallway at a medium pace, thoughts racing through her head. In her mind, she recalled how this had all begun. She remembered how the first Ironborn had been spontaneously created nearly eight years ago. After the change, the being had destroyed the iron refinery he was at, hence the species name. Others like the first had then started appearing all over the globe.

The Ironborn. A species that was more advanced than normal humans in almost every way. Not only were they stronger, smarter, and faster than humans, but they also occasionally had strange and unnatural abilities ranging from teleportation to supernatural beauty. No one knew their origin nor the extent of their powers, only that any abilities they obtained after becoming Ironborn would often, but not always, reflect their natural talents.

At first, the Ironborn lived in society like normal people. And, like normal people, some were good and some were bad. However, they had greater power than normal humans, allowing them to do much more. Any part of the human before becoming Ironborn would improve, making them faster, stronger, smarter, and better looking. Any talent that the human had would be supersized, allowing them to perform inhuman acts of mystifying power.

Due to their improved state, they began to rise up the ranks in the world. Nearly all celebrities were moved out as better-looking Ironborn took their place. The government seats began to be filled by the superhumans due to their higher intelligence and strategic minds. Athletes and sports stars also got replaced by the Ironborn, who outmatched even the best of humans.

People began to feel uneasy. They were not used to having a species that was superior to them. It was different. It made them uncomfortable to have an entire species that they could never surpass. So they began to react.

Some humans began to organize gangs that would attack, molest and kill the Ironborn. It was much harder to kill an Ironborn than a normal person, but it was far from impossible. Ironborn may have been stronger, but they were hopelessly outnumbered, even with the support of the humans who were kind to them, who began to refer to themselves as the Red Army.

Eventually, a billionaire named David Cadmore had come up with an idea to stop this. He was an Ironborn whose abilities allowed him incredible technical talent and smarts. Using his abilities, he gained Ironborn followers and gave them weapons and technology that he had built in order to protect themselves and others. This then grew to become an army. David made Cadmore Industries, a network of weapon-building factories to support the soldiers. Cadmore Industries' plan succeeded, and the Ironborn were sufficiently protected, but it did not stop there.

David and an Ironborn programmer named Caleb Griffin had gotten together and created what they called Enforcement. Enforcement was an army of fighting robots that were used to replace the Ironborn soldiers, making it so that the Ironborn no longer had to risk their lives, as the robots fought for them. Enforcement had helicopters, jeeps, planes and tanks. Even before the Enforcement had done anything, their existence was intimidating enough to scare any opposing sides. The gangs began to back off, and the Ironborn began to live fully again.

All was going well until one summer night David Cadmore died, and the world flipped upside down. Dr. Griffin, who had never been known to be the most sane person, became the new owner of the industry, and turned the Enforcement against the Ironborn.

In the next few days following the turn of the industry, millions of Ironborn were killed. This day had been named The Purge. Nearly all of the Ironborn died, and those that didn't were now in hiding.

Nobody expected this to happen, so nobody was prepared. Nobody, that was, except for the Ironborn warrior. The Ironborn warrior was an Ironborn of great power and intelligence. He foresaw the fall of Cadmore Industries and created a backup plan. The Ironborn Protection Agency.

The IPA was a new army of Ironborn, led by the Ironborn warrior. For a while, the IPA prepared and trained, waiting until they were strong enough to intervene. Eventually the time came, and the war over Cadmore Industries had begun.

Now, three years after The Purge, Cadmore Industries and the IPA were still at war. No one knew how long it would be until the end of the fighting. No one knew-

Talia's thoughts were cut off by voices in front of her. She had headed to a meeting to report her efforts in the war, and she had now arrived. She recognized the voice she heard as Captain Dax's, the highest-ranking officer from another clan.

"Why should we trust you with this mission?" Talia heard from behind the door. "Our own troops are strong enough on their own."

"Because you have no other choice." That was a voice Talia knew well. It was the voice of her own clan leader, Captain Vilo. Vilo was a good captain, but was often too arrogant to realize her mistakes. It wasn't a wonder that she and the impulsive Captain Dax never got along. "All of the other clans have their own matters to deal with other than Duo, and they will never come to your aid. Anaki is your best ally but they haven't been strong enough since the battle of the Flaming Hill. You need help from us because you are out of options."

"And yet the past shows that your clan is insufficient for our needs," he said. "Project 1697 is an important mission. I trusted that assignment with Sergeant Bi and her *squad* of soldiers," he said in a mocking tone. "What is the news on them? If there were no delays, as you promised, they should be back by now."

"That they are," Talia said as she opened the door. The room had a long, black metal table lined with chairs seating many of Clan Vilo's high-ranking officers. Talia recognized the unique badges and armor of den commanders Exon, Lan and Mark seated around the table, along with many other squad sergeants like herself. Clan Captain Vilo sat at the head of the table next to a holographic projection of Captain Dax. Everyone in the room that was not a sergeant, which was the lowest rank other than soldiers, wore their helmets. It was a sign of respect that no one of a lower rank knew the identity of their leaders.

"Look who has finally shown up," Dax mocked.

"Perfectly on time, mind you," Talia said, taking a seat near the door. "And may I add the fact that we received none of the promised aid in defeating our enemies."

Dax sniffed. "We had other matters to deal with. Besides, Project 1697 is not in my clan anyway. You will be taking him."

This had been expected but it was still unacceptable. The only reason he didn't want Cago is because he was small. Small, unlike the rest of Clan Dax, who specialized in heavyweight and strength. Talia gritted her teeth, "I don't know if you realize this, but Project 1697 is a human being. You can't just throw him away like a piece of garbage. Do you not-"

"Bi," Vilo cut in, using her sergeant name, "You are in no position or authority to question the judgment of a clan captain. 1697 will be your responsibility now." She turned. "Captain Dax, you may leave." Dax signed off and his holographic image flickered away. She turned back to Talia. "I don't want this to happen either, but we are under no position to argue with Dax. As much as I hate his judgment, we are on the same side."

Talia was about to respond when Commander Mark spoke up, "Sir, incoming transmission from Clan Pris."

"Let them through," Vilo said.

A hologram flickered to life beside Vilo, and a person covered in armor appeared, "Captain Vilo, I am Commander Venus."

"Commander, where is your captain?" Vilo asked.

"On the front lines, as always," Venus said.

Vilo shook her head. "Very well."

"I also have pressing matters to attend to," he continued. "Sergeant Andromeda will give you the rundown of our current situation." He turned and left, his body phasing into static before vanishing entirely as he walked out of the hologram's projection.

Things up there must be bad if a squad sergeant is giving the report, Talia thought. Captain Pris was *always* fighting on the front lines, but not even having a commander to run the base? That must be intense.

Sergeant Andromeda walked into the hologram's view. Seeing that no one at the meeting was a lower rank than her, she removed her helmet. She had long, straight blonde hair and bright blue eyes. She was young as well, about Talia's age. She pressed a button on the table in front of her and a three-dimensional image of the Manhattan skyline appeared. "Our soldiers have recently been stationed in these three towers, firing down at the enemies from a distance." Three of the buildings turned red. "We have to move our position every once and a while so the enemy doesn't catch us. It only takes them a matter of hours to find us before we are again forced to relocate."

"Is Pris sure that she doesn't want our support?" Vilo asked.

"Yes," Andromeda said. "We have been able to handle it up to this point and our Clan Captain believes that-"

Suddenly the holographic image began to become scratchy as Andromeda glitched for a moment before disappearing. Bi saw Vilo's posture tense.

"What happened?" Vilo asked, turning to Den Commander Mark.

"Their systems have gone offline," Mark said.

"Well then get them back on!" Vilo commanded.

The room went into chaos for a moment as the commanders and sergeants used their small electronic tablets to try and figure out what the issue was.

"I've found something!" Commander Exon shouted, quieting everyone. "A distress signal from one of the other outposts. Andromeda's tower has fallen!"

Vilo looked over at him, her voice stern. "Casualties?"

"Unknown, but they believe there are some survivors," he replied. "They are now requesting backup."

Vilo's head slowly turned to Bi. "Well, seeing as you think you're the smartest in the room, why don't you go test your skills by aiding the efforts in New York?"

All eyes turned to her as Talia paused for a moment. She knew that her squad was considered the least experienced because of how young they were. They weren't giving her a chance to prove herself. They just all knew that going to New York would be extremely dangerous. But backing down would not lead Bi to success.

So now my group matters, Talia thought. But she simply nodded and replied. "What of the boy?"

"Take him with you," Vilo replied. "You are to train him and welcome him into your squad."

Talia hesitated before standing up and turning to leave.

"Bi," Vilo said again. She turned. "Try to stay alive. We need you out there."

Talia smiled. "I know."

4-Initiation

The Warehouse, Outside of Sacramento
California, USA
8:30 p.m.
Flynn

"Right away, sergeant," Flynn said into his wrist comm link. He walked down the hallway towards the front room of the warehouse. He then opened the door, walked through, and turned towards the scrawny boy who was sitting on the couch. Cago.

Cago would be the first member in this squad that Flynn had known before the war. Flynn and Cago had been friends for more than two years now, since the beginning of eighth grade. Of course, Cago did not know that the soldier in front of him was his friend because of Flynn's suit and helmet, which was obscuring his face.

Cago was shorter than Flynn and younger too, by a couple of months. His mother had been from Taiwan and his father... Well, Flynn didn't know. He had left Cago's family right before Flynn met him, and no one had heard from him since. The only thing that Cago still had from his father was a four-inch knife that hung from a chain around his neck, which he had been given the day his dad had left. His mother had died about a year later, and he had moved in with his only surviving relative. His aunt. And now she was gone too.

"Project 1697," Flynn said. Cago looked up. "I just got word from Squad Sergeant Bi that you are now going to be in our squad. Like usual, Clan Captain Dax decided not to allow you in, so you are now going to be with us."

"Who is Clan Captain Dax?" Cago asked.

"One of the leaders of this organization," Flynn gestured to the warehouse around him, "The highest-ranking leader of our organization, the Ironborn Protection Agency or IPA, is the Ironborn Warrior. We call him Mr. Z. Beneath him are the clan captains, like Captain Dax. In each clan there are three dens, and each den has a commander. Under that, there are typically three squad sergeants, like Bi, each one directing their own squad. Make sense?"

Cago nodded hesitantly, processing the information.

"You will get it all eventually," Flynn continued. "There are seven different clans here in the IPA. They all are better at different things based on who and where they are, which also helps us work better together when fighting against the Industry. Clan Dax is best at brute strength, which is helpful due to their common street fights with gangs and groups of Enforcement. They are stationed in southern California.

"Clan Neo is in Utah. They are fashioned the most like an army, having full-scale battles and occasionally assisting in combat with organizations that support Ironborn in other countries around the world. Clan Pris is in New York. They specialize in long-range combat, which helps them due to the only safe place being high in the upper stories of skyscrapers. Clan Duo is in Texas, along with Hawaii and the American-owned islands. They are assassin-like melee soldiers, which helps them in the jungles of Hawaii and against the stealth troops that they often fight against. Xion is in Minnesota. They are the ones that build all of our technology, which is manufactured in the dozens of factories we have there. Troy is in Florida. They are the most elite clan. The best soldiers from each clan are taken and put through vigorous training in order to be in Clan Troy. They are also in charge of the Redstone Project, which is the group that is trying to find and destroy the Cadmore Industries headquarters. Bi has tried to get in multiple times, but they haven't accepted her yet."

"Finally, there is Clan Vilo. That is where you and I come in. Vilo is the support clan. We are, of course, stationed in northern California, but due to Clan Dax being so close, we often go around and help out the other clans. You got that?"

Cago looked at him with wide eyes as he spoke. "Kind of," He spoke slowly, as if trying to create a mental list in his brain. "I have tried to research the IPA in the past, but there isn't a ton of accurate information on you guys." He said slowly, "So why aren't we helping in the war right now?"

"We are a junior squad," Flynn explained, "All of us here are young, so we mainly just train and research projects. Projects are people like you. People that we suspect may have abilities."

"So there are 1697 members of the IPA?" Cago asked.

"Give or take a few, considering some are still pending, " Flynn answered. "I myself was project 971. Of course, if a project turns out negative, the number is assigned to a new suspect."

"So how long are we in a junior squad?" Cago inquired.

"Until we are eighteen," Flynn said. "Then we get to move on and actually fight. Hopefully the war will be over by then, but if we need to fight, we will." He paused again. "Speaking of which, I should probably introduce you to the rest of the group. The first person you should meet is me. The people here have given me the nickname of Scorpius." Flynn pressed a button on his neck and his helmet collapsed into his suit. "But my real name is Flynn."

Cago stood up in surprise. "Flynn?"

Flynn smiled. "Didn't recognize me?"

"Not at all," he said, still surprised.

"Well, the suits have very good voice scramblers," Flynn replied.

"Not just that," Cago said. "Flynn, I've known you for years, and I would have never guessed that you had powers. You must have hidden it really well."

"So did you," Flynn noted.

"I guess," Cago said. "I have only had my powers for two years though. Probably not as long as you."

"Wait," Flynn said, beginning to piece things together. "Two years ago was when..."

"Yeah," Cago said, looking down at the ground. "My dad was the leader of a major gang against the Ironborn. When he found out that his son was one of them, he just... poof." He mimed with his hands. He paused for a second before attempting to change the subject. "So how do you get to school?"

"The bus," Flynn answered simply. "Besides, Tarff and Blackeye can drive."

"Tarff?" Cago asked.

"A member of our squad," Flynn explained. "I mean with four arms it would be kind of sad if you couldn't drive."

"Four arms?" Cago asked.

"Do you want to meet him?" Flynn asked.

"Sure." Cago followed Flynn out of the front room, and into a hallway. Flynn turned and opened a door to his left and looked inside. The interior of the room was fairly large, and reminded Cago of a beach. The ground was hardwood, and the walls a deep blue. The only things in the room besides a bed was a ukulele on a nightstand and a small tan wicker rug.

"He isn't here," Flynn said. "It's fine. We can find him later."

Flynn continued leading Cago down the hall, through a door and out into a massive, high ceilinged garage full of half-finished projects, vehicles, tools, and piles of scrap metal. Loud alternative rock music was playing from a speaker in the middle of the garage. Next to the speaker was a person, kneeling on the ground. He was wearing a welding mask and was fixing some piece of machinery, orange sparks spraying out from both sides of his work area.

Flynn led Cago through the minefield of things until they reached the boy. Flynn then reached down and turned off the speaker.

The person stopped welding, flipping up his mask, "Zane, for the last time, stop turning-" He paused when he saw who it was. "Oh, it's you." He pressed a button on his wrist controller, causing his welding mask, chest cover, and gloves to collapse down, disappearing and leaving him in a T-shirt and khaki pants. He had long, shaggy blonde hair, and seemed like the kind of guy that had spent all day surfing for his entire life. Cago had also noticed that the glove on his right hand was missing two fingers, and those same fingers on his hand were glowing softly. He wondered if that meant the fingers themselves had been the ones welding.

"Cago," Flynn said, "this is Ryan."

"What's up?" He shook Cago's hand loosely. "I'm the engineer and co-pilot for our squad."

"Pilot? Why do you need a pilot?" Cago asked.

"For the Rizen of course," Ryan said as if he should understand. When Cago stared at him blankly, he turned to Flynn. "Seriously Flynn, you were supposed to give him an initiation. What did you do? Tell him about random things that aren't important?"

"I thought you would want to show him the *cool* stuff."

Ryan paused. "I didn't think about that, but yes. Cago, let me show you the *cool* stuff." He began to lead Cago farther into what he could now see was an L-shaped garage. Ryan first pointed out three vehicles that sat in a line in front of one garage door. "These are my babies. A Calillac Escalade, a Ford Raptor, and a Lamborghini Aventador. From the outside, they are all perfect replicas, but Clan Xion, along with my own personal modifications, have made them more than battle worthy." They continued walking, and when they turned around the corner, the three boys stopped.

"Cago," Ryan said, "this is my pride and joy, the Rizen."

Cago took a few steps back, almost tripping over a pile of metal. In front of them, towering nearly to the top of the two-story high ceiling, was a matte-black aerospace craft.

"Wait," Cago hesitated, confused. "Isn't that an Enforcement vehicle?"

Ryan looked at Flynn in approval. "This kid knows his stuff." He said, turning back to Cago. "This is a B-12 Cadmore Industries armed airborne troop carrier. Blackeye was the one who shot it down. When we asked if we could fix it up and use it, nobody had objections, so we did. It was part of the Horizon squad, but some of the letters were scratched off, so we renamed it."

"Blackeye? He sounds scary."

Ryan turned to Flynn. "You haven't introduced him to Blackeye yet? I want to see that," he said with a chuckle.

"Who is he?" Cago asked.

Flynn turned to Cago. "First of all, it's a *she*. She's our long-range specialist. She never talks to anyone though. Or takes off her helmet in front of others. Or her suit. We don't know why."

"I know why," Ryan said astutely, "She doesn't talk to anyone she doesn't think is intelligent. That includes all boys, apparently. In fact, the only one she has ever talked to, that we know of, is Bi."

"She sounds like every girl I try to talk to," Cago joked, "How do you know it's a girl if you've never seen her face or talked to her?"

"Oh trust me, it's obvious," Ryan said.

Flynn slapped him on the arm.

"What?" Ryan asked defensively.

Flynn shook his head and turned back to Cago, "We know she's a girl because Bi uses the pronoun 'she' while speaking about her."

"Hey, I'm still right," Ryan said.

"Well, that doesn't happen every day," Flynn countered.

Ryan folded his arms, "Sure it does."

"Speaking of intelligence," Flynn joked, "Where is Zane?"

"Wow Flynn," Ryan said, smiling. "Just because of that, I won't tell you."

"Fine." Flynn turned and beckoned Cago to follow him.

"Is that how all of your conversations go?" Cago asked him.

"Pretty much. I can't even remember the last time Ryan was in a serious mood." Flynn ducked as they walked underneath the Rizen and towards a door on the other side of the garage.

"Are there any other projects at our school?" Cago said.

"Yes," Flynn said. He opened the door, which led into a small office. "In fact, I think that we will be looking into Project 1711 next."

"Yeah, you wish," A voice said. At first, Cago turned around to see if it was Ryan who had spoken. The voice sounded just like his. It took him a moment to figure out that the voice had come from inside the office.

"Cago," Flynn said, "This is Nerd. He is our tech specialist and pilot."

"My name's Zane, although I will gratefully take 'nerd' as a compliment, Flynn." He said without looking up from his computer. His hair was short and combed neatly, but his face looked just like Ryan's. He wore a button-up shirt and had headphones around his neck. "I'm the squad's computer technician, programmer, and pilot. If you need upgrades to your suits and weapons, you come to me. I also program the robots that Ryan builds." He spoke as if he was reading a script.

"Who's 1711?" Cago asked him.

"No one," Flynn said quickly.

"Oh, it's just some girl," Zane said offhandedly.

"Any girl in particular?" Cago asked, turning slowly to look at Flynn.

"We're getting off topic," Flynn said. "Zane, Cago needs to be put into the system."

"Right," Zane said, still typing. "It's Project 1697 right?"

"That's the one," Flynn affirmed.

The computer's keyboard clacked for a moment. "Perfect," Zane said. "You're in the system."

"Thanks Zane." Flynn led Cago out of the office.

"So..." Cago said, "Will you ever tell me who this 1711 is?"

"Eventually," Flynn replied.

"Have I met her?" he inquired.

"Doesn't matter."

"Come on," he complained. "At least tell me if I've met her."

Flynn paused for a while, trying to figure out if Cago was playing with him. He most likely had already guessed it was Emily. "Yes, you've met her."

He pushed open the door in front of them and walked into a large kitchen. Standing at the counter, spreading peanut butter on about ten different pieces of bread, was a huge, seven foot tall Polynesian man with four arms. The butter knife he was holding looked like a toothpick in his hand. He was wearing a dark blue button-up T-shirt with pink flowers and a tupenu to match. He smiled kindly as they approached him.

"Cago, this is Tarff. Our heavyweight."

"Hello little man," he smiled as he gazed down at Cago. His voice was so deep that Flynn could feel it through his entire body. Tarff seemed like the type of guy who was really nice, but could also pound you into applesauce if you faced him in a football game. He picked up one of the sandwiches and began eating it. "My full name is Tarff'antu'loga Anu'manu'taki, but you can call me Tarff."

"Hello," Cago shook one of his massive hands.

"I am also the group chef," he said.

"How come you're so tall?" Cago asked.

Tarff chuckled as he took a bite of sandwich, "It's a hereditary thing. This may surprise you, but I am actually the smallest of all of my older brothers and cousins." He finished his sandwich and picked up another one. "Inhuman strength has run in our specific tribe since long before the Ironborn came."

"And so have long names," Flynn mumbled.

"Me and all of my relatives all happened to get powers too. Most of them are in Clan Dax. They actually make up the entirety of the Anu'manu'taki squad. I was just too small so I got put here, in the support clan." His words were jumbled around mouthfuls of food as he finished his second sandwich and picked up another one.

"Too small," Cago scoffed.

"Not as small as you." Tarff noted. "You'd be a great stealth trooper. Blackeye might have a little bit of competition."

"Speaking of Blackeye," Flynn said. "We now only have one more person to meet." He left the kitchen and went back into the front room, Cago following close behind. He then led him back into the first hallway near Tarff's bedroom before turning to walk up a flight of stairs. When they reached the top, they began walking down a hallway lined with doors.

"These are our rooms," Flynn explained. He turned to his left and knocked on a door. No response came, but he opened it. "Cago, this is Blackeye."

They entered the room and found Blackeye in her full suit and helmet, sitting cross-legged on her bed, using a rag to clean her sniper rifle. He could almost feel her gaze piercing into him.

"She is our long-range specialist and our healer," Flynn continued.

She nodded towards them. Then Flynn turned and left, shutting the door behind him.

"That's it?" Cago asked, following him farther down the hallway.

"Be glad she gave you any recognition at all," Flynn said. "I think she might kind of like you."

"Why doesn't she talk to anyone?" he asked.

"We don't know for sure," Flynn answered. "Ryan thinks that she just hates our guts, but according to Bi she's had a lot of bad things happen to her. She finds it hard to trust people."

"Oh," Cago said, not knowing how else to respond.

Flynn turned and opened another door. "Here is your room. It isn't much, but you can add anything you'd like once we have more time."

Cago looked inside at the bland bedroom, which contained only a bed and a small dresser. "It's much better than the one I had at my aunt's apartment." He turned back to Flynn, "You never told me what their powers are."

"So I didn't." Flynn thought for a moment. "Well, Blackeye has healing and sight abilities, Zane can do crazy things with technology and computers, Ryan is the same as Zane but with his engineering skills, Bi is insanely intelligent, and I have telekinetic powers."

"What do you mean by crazy things with technology?" Cago inquired.

"It just makes sense to him I suppose," Flynn responded. "Lots of Ironborn don't have specific powers, just advancements of their normal talents. Others, like me, have both. My strength, speed, and intelligence have also been enhanced, along with the abilities I have received. Zane and Ryan have explained that their abilities work in a way where they don't need to learn how to do something in their areas of expertise, they just see the problem and automatically know what to do."

"What about the Samoan?" Cago asked.

Flynn's eyes grew wide and he looked over his shoulder, as if checking for something. He turned back to Cago. "It's a good thing he didn't hear that. Tarff is the friendliest guy I know, but when someone calls him a Samoan, his Tongan side comes out in full force."

"Oh," Cago shuddered. "I definitely do not want to see Tarff angry."

Flynn smiled, "No, you don't. Especially considering that his powers have to do with strength. When he uses them, he can grow in size and power considerably, and even become invincible for short periods of time. He also, of course, has four arms, but he can retract those into his body when trying to look like a normal human. He is essentially the reason that his high school has won the state championship in football three years in a row." He paused. "What powers do you have?"

Cago scratched behind his ear. "I can extinguish lights, make areas colder, make it harder for people to see, and lots of other things that have to do with darkness. If it is dark enough, I can even turn invisible."

Flynn nodded. "Well, our first goal will be to help you be able to control and use your powers to the best of your ability. Speaking of which, there is actually one more place I want to show you. Come on."

Flynn led Cago out of the room and down the hall. They went back through the kitchen and out into the garage, right next to Zane's office. Flynn pulled open a door and ushered Cago inside.

The interior was a large, plain white room with a high rise ceiling. The only thing in the room was a pile of large metal crates in one corner and a row of what looked like lockers.

"What is this room for?" Cago inquired.

"This is, personally, is my favorite room in the warehouse," Flynn answered. "The training room." Flynn led him over to the lockers and opened one. Inside was what looked like a bunch of fake knives and laser tag equipment.

"Take your pick," he said, gesturing to the shelves.

Cago grabbed a short combat knife, similar to the one on the chain around his neck.

"That's it?" Flynn asked. Cago shrugged.

They stepped back to the middle of the room. "Watch this." Flynn looked up. "Proxy?"

"Yes?" The artificial female voice sounded like it was coming from all directions, making Cago jump a little.

"Start system fifty two."

Suddenly the lights in the room turned off. Cago, of course, could see in the dark, and he watched as the doors to some of the lockers opened and humanoid robots stepped out, taking positions around the room. The crates moved too, sliding across the ground and into new formations.

The lights turned back on, but this time the room looked much different. He was in what looked like an alley now, the brick walls on either side rising much higher than the ceiling of the room had been just moments before.

He heard noises coming from behind the dumpster to his right and saw a figure in black jump toward him. Acting out of pure instinct, he tried to stop the attack with the fake knife in his hand. To his surprise, it pierced the skin of his attacker, sending him to the ground.

Cago tried to remember how many robots he had seen in the darkness. Seven? Possibly eight?

His thoughts were cut off as another cloaked figure dropped from above, catching him off guard as two more came out from the shadows.

Cago dodged a punch from the first attacker before retaliating, cutting him with his knife before turning to the other two. Before he could do anything, he was grabbed from behind. The grip was extremely tight, but the hand felt like a human, nothing like the robotic hands that he had seen.

Jerking himself out of the robot's grasp, Cago dove into a pocket of shadow, disappearing from view. He counted the amount of robots still left in the alleyway and cursed. Nine.

Quickly devising a plan, Cago hopped on top of a metal crate designed to look like a trash can, cutting the neck of one robot as he leapt towards another. The attackers looked disoriented as he flashed in and out of their view, taking them out one by one.

Finding a metal pipe on the ground, Cago picked it up and bashed it into the head of another enemy before throwing his knife across the alley, downing the final attacker.

The image flickered before disappearing, fading back to a solid white room. He saw Flynn standing a few feet away, clapping slowly. "Very well done."

"You could have told me what was going to happen," Cago said, trying to catch his breath.

"Well, that's something you'll learn about us very quickly," he responded. "We're full of surprises."

The robots got up from the ground and mechanically walked back into their lockers. "That was cool," Cago said. "How did you guys make this?"

"Clan Xion built it before our squad was assigned here," Flynn said. "It has some of their nicest technology. The ironbots are made by Ryan though. We also take them into battle. The IPA has tons of them."

“I think I saw some of them during your fight yesterday,” Cago said. The room had now completely reset to its former position.

A light on Flynn’s wrist began flashing, and he glanced down at it. “Sergeant Bi has returned,” he said, “Let’s see what she has to say to us.”

5- Preparations

The Warehouse, Outside of Sacramento
California, USA
9:30 p.m.
Flynn

When Bi entered the warehouse, everyone was waiting in the front room, sitting on the various couches or standing against the walls. They looked up as she walked into the room.

"Did I miss something?" she asked as she walked past them, setting her purse down on the unused receptionist desk.

"Don't you have news for us?" Flynn inquired.

"Who said that?" she asked, fake curiosity on her face.

Flynn looked at her. "Bi-"

"I was joking," Bi said. "All of you always have so much tension." She looked around for a moment and took a deep breath. "I got word from Captain Vilo while at our meeting. We are going to help Clan Pris in the war of New York." Everyone looked surprised. "They lost one of their outposts and are now in great need of our assistance."

"How long do we have?" Ryan asked.

"Three hours."

"Are we taking the Rizen?" Zane inquired.

"It's the only way to get there fast enough. You and Ryan will need to get it prepared." Bi turned to Flynn. "Get Cago some gear and fill him in with the needed information about Clan Pris. Tarff, load our equipment onto the Rizen. Proxy?"

"Yes?" said the artificial female voice from the ceiling speakers.

"Prepare the warehouse for temporary lockdown."

"Starting lockdown procedures now," Proxy responded.

"Blackeye, come with me to prepare our equipment," Bi said as she walked out of the room.

As everyone split up to do their separate tasks, Flynn led Cago through the main hallway, out into the garage, and to a room in the far corner of the warehouse. He opened the door. "This," he said, "Is the armory." The room was large and had tons of weapons lining the walls. There were guns, swords, grenades, and other random pieces of equipment which were organized on shelves and hooks. Flynn led Cago to the back where he pulled a small box out from where it sat in a small canister-like hole in the wall, along with a black utility belt. "Take these."

"What are they?" Cago asked.

"This may not look like much, but it will save your life," Flynn said, attaching the box to the belt. "Put it on."

Cago slid the belt around his waist. "Now what?"

"Watch this." Flynn reached over and pressed a button on the box. Instantly, a suit spread itself around Cago's body, its hexagonal design rippling as it fit his scrawny build.

"Wow," Cago's voice was now distorted by his helmet. It sounded raspy and crazed, nothing like his normal quiet voice. "Bi had one of these on when she took me here. What is it?"

"It," Flynn responded, "is the best technology in the world, built by the engineers at Clan Xion. This may not feel like much more than a wet suit, but it can stop a bullet."

"Really?"

Flynn pulled a small pistol from the wall, pointed it at Cago, and pulled the trigger. Cago flinched, but the bullet bounced off him harmlessly.

"You could have warned me before you did that!" Cago exclaimed.

"Our enemies won't give any warnings," Flynn said. "Besides, that suit can block a lot more than a simple .44 bullet. These suits also give you extra strength. You can jump higher, run faster, lift more, and pack a little extra damage into your punch." Flynn put the gun back. "Now all you need is some weapons."

"My knife is all I need," Cago said.

Flynn chuckled, "Are you sure?"

"This knife has saved my life multiple times," he added.

"I think I know what you mean." Flynn reached out his hand.

"What are you doing?" Cago asked, confused.

"Wait for it," Flynn said. After a few seconds, his mataka flew through the doorway and onto its mount on his forearm and his hiveblade flew into his other hand.

Cago's eyes went wide with surprise. "How did you do that?"

"My powers," Flynn explained. "Bi helped me develop my abilities to be able to locate my weapons and use my powers to gravitate them towards myself." He chuckled. "When I'm indoors it takes a lot more effort than you might imagine."

Cago looked at him curiously. "Couldn't you use your powers to stop blood from leaving your body if you get injured?"

"I don't think I would be able to focus hard enough to influence the individual blood vessels in my body without locking up an entire organ or limb. Especially in the center of battle," Flynn replied. "Besides, I prefer to prevent getting wounds by using this." He smiled and held up his mataka. "I have used these weapons for years. My grandfather was an archeologist, and found them in far east Asia. I inherited them from my grandfather after he died."

"And they work against Enforcement soldiers?" Cago inquired.

"By themselves, they would shatter against the armor of an Enforcement robot." Flynn said with a chuckle. "Zane had to reinforce them with Clan Xion's custom metal, Dragon Steel. The same stuff that is used in nearly all of our equipment. It is very light, yet extremely durable." He set the tip of his hiveblade on the ground. "These weapons have saved my life many times, and have killed many enemies, but there have also been many times when Enforcement has been too far away, even if I throw my mataka. That is when a long-range weapon comes in handy." He pulled a black gun off of a shelf. "This is a seventy caliber triple shot semi auto rifle. It is very similar to the one I have used for years now as my sidearm."

Cago took the weapon. "Isn't seventy caliber a lot?"

"Without a suit, or without being Ironborn, using it could seriously damage your arm, but with our suits, you won't feel a thing," Flynn said. "Besides, this thing would be massive and very heavy if Clan Xion hadn't found a way to condense it."

Cago put the gun back on the shelf. "Still seems a bit too large for me."

"Well, it's not like you don't have other choices." Flynn motioned to the room around them. "Take your pick."

Tarff heaved another box onto the Rizen. "You got that gun fixed yet, Ryan?"

"Almost," A voice said from underneath the aircraft as another spray of sparks blasted out onto the cement floor.

"Twenty minutes until the lockdown sequence is complete," Proxy announced.

Ryan came out from underneath the ship. "The gun should work now." He removed his gloves and disengaged his welding mask. "You have spare ammo loaded?"

Tarff nodded. "Zane already prepped the guns. Bi doesn't think we will have much trouble landing in New York. Being in the streets tends to be the harder part of the trip." He lifted another metal crate and walked up the gangway into the back of the Rizen.

"Think you'll be alright on the flight?" Ryan asked.

Tarff shrugged. "Bi has helped me train for heights so I think I'll be fine. Although I would much rather be on land or water than flying through the air. In my mind, humans were never meant to be like birds."

Ryan went to one of the smaller boxes that was still on the ground and, after struggling to lift it, slowly shuffled it up the gangway. After making it about halfway, he stopped for a break.

"And I don't think you were ever meant to be a heavyweight," Tarff said with a chuckle as he walked past, easily using one hand to lift the crate that Ryan had been carrying. "Maybe you should go help Bi. I can finish these."

"That sounds like a good idea," Ryan responded, breathing heavily with his hands on his knees for a few seconds before he straightened up and exited the garage.

Tarff entered the ship's cargo bay and set the crate down with the others. He looked around. The inside of the ship was large, and consisted of four rooms with bunk beds along a main hallway that led to a large frontal cockpit. It had two autoloader cannons attached on the front of the ship, barely glanceable from the front where Tarff was standing, and one beneath the ship, meaning it could take and deal considerable damage in a fight without falling out of the sky.

Stepping down the gangway and back out into the garage, Tarff began loading the rest of the crates back into the cargo bay. After a few minutes, Bi, Zane and Ryan entered and loaded their own gear onto the ship. After a short time came Blackeye and finally Flynn and Cago.

"Everything loaded?" Bi asked Tarff.

"Ready when you are," Tarff confirmed.

"Proxy?"

"Lockdown sequence on stand by," the computer said.

The squad filed into the ship. Zane and Ryan, being the pilots, sat in the front as everyone else got into the passenger seats.

Zane flipped some switches on the dashboard and the engines began to hum softly. He then pressed a button that opened the large door in the back of the garage. Steering the ship forwards, Zane pulled the Rizen out of the warehouse.

"Proxy, complete lockdown," Bi said

Looking out the side window of the Rizen, Tarff could see the garage door close as they flew away into the overcast sky.

6- Pawn

The Rizen
Somewhere above the U.S.
10:00 p.m.
Flynn

From his seat behind Zane, Flynn could peer down over their shoulder and look out the front window of the Rizen to watch the clouds pass in a blur beneath him. Out of the corner of his eye, he saw Ryan walk up behind Bi, who was leaning against the far wall, eyes fixated on something in the distance through the window.

"I got the problem fixed," Ryan said. "The navigation computer is up and running."

"Nice work," Bi replied.

Flynn turned and began walking down the hallway from the front of the ship to the back. He approached a door on his right and knocked.

"Come in," Cago's voice said.

Flynn entered. "Are you doing all right?"

"Just a little disoriented, that's all," Cago said. He was sitting on the edge of a bunk bed, the slightest bit of tiredness in his eyes, like always. "It has been a little crazy recently, as you know."

Flynn nodded. “Well if you need anything, just let me know. I’ll be on the bridge.” He started walking away.

“Flynn?”

He turned back around.

“Have you ever met someone from this clan we’re going to?” Cago asked. “I don’t remember the name, was it Priss?”

“First of all, the ‘S’ in the name ‘Pris’ is silent. It’s pronounced Pree, not Priss.”

“Oh.”

“But, yes, I have met a squad from Clan Pris. Why?”

“Just curious.”

“The people from Pris are typically respected by the rest of the IPA.” Flynn said. “It’s Dax and Duo who don’t like us.”

“Why is that?” Cago inquired.

“Rumor says that Vilo and Captain Dax have had it out for each other since even before this war began, and the only things I’ve heard about Duo is that their fighting techniques can be... interesting,” Flynn said.

“Oh ok,” Cago responded.

Flynn’s wrist comm began flashing. “The sergeant wants me. Try and get some sleep.” He turned and exited into the hall, the metal door sliding closed behind him.

Now that Cago was in the squad with him, investigating projects from his school would be twice as easy. Not that it would help much, of course, because the only current project at his school was Emily. Someone that Flynn had not considered restraining from telling people the identity of until Cago had showed up. Everyone else in the squad just made jokes about it and moved on, but Cago actually knew who she was. Thinking of her began to make Flynn worried. He was so far away from her right now. What if something happened to her while he was gone?

Flynn opened a door at the end of the hall and entered the back section of the cockpit. The area was large, with seating for the entire squad, multiple storage closets, and a hologram display table near the back.

Bi was at the display table looking at a holographic map of New York when Flynn entered. The ship was currently on autopilot, and everyone else seemed to have gone to bed for the hour or two they had before they would land.

Bi smiled lightly as he walked in. "Hello Flynn."

"You wanted to see me?" He asked.

"Yes." Bi studied his face.

"What?" Flynn asked.

Bi smiled, "You're worried about her."

“Who?” Flynn asked. He had never told Bi about how he felt for Emily. He had always tried to sound all business when reporting any new information on her.

“We both know who I’m talking about.” Bi said, turning back to the map of the buildings. “Project 1711, or as you know her, Emily Sharp.”

Flynn blinked in surprise. “How did-”

“Come on, Flynn,” she said. She swiped her finger on a screen and her view of the map shifted positions, moving to a different sector of the city. “You have known me for nearly three years now and you still don’t know that I have a knack for figuring things out?”

Flynn sighed. “Alright, fine. Yes, I’m worried about Emily. She has been showing many signs of being Ironborn, and with us gone, now would be the perfect time for Enforcement to move in.”

“That may be true,” Bi said, “but worrying is not going to save her.” She looked up at him. “Flynn, you have to promise me that you won’t let your feelings get in the way of your capabilities to fight in this war. It is going to be very dangerous these next few days. You are an extremely capable soldier, Flynn, but if your emotions are too strong, you may end up hurting yourself or compromising our mission. Do you understand?”

Flynn looked down. “Yes sergeant.”

Bi sighed. "I know what it's like, Flynn. I know how it feels to be worried about them, especially in the middle of a war." Her eyes were lost in thought for a moment.

"Who is he?" Flynn asked. Bi occasionally spoke of this person she knew before the war, but never gave anything specific.

Bi smiled. "He is amazing, that's what he is. He was strong, handsome, witty, and intelligent." She paused on that last word. "He was the only person that I couldn't seem to outsmart. The only person who could get me distracted, to make me lose my focus. It was a new feeling that I had never experienced before." She turned back to Flynn. "Of course, that also could have proven hazardous once the war came, had we both not figured out how to control our emotions." She paused again. "Maybe someday, after the war, you will be able to meet him."

Flynn smiled. "I would like that."

Bi was silent for a moment. "Flynn, while we're on this subject, I wanted to teach you something. That is the importance of worth. Emily may be very important to you, but you must not waste other precious things to save her. Let me give you an example." She pulled an object out of her pocket. It was a small wooden chess piece, elegantly carved with great detail. "What is this?"

"A pawn," Flynn responded.

"Well, let's say that this isn't any ordinary pawn," Bi said. "This pawn is very important to you. During a match, it happened to save your king from imminent death. So, let's now say that later in that same match, this pawn becomes in danger. Because you favor this pawn above others, you move in with your queen to save it. Your queen dies, but your pawn lives." She paused. "Until your opponent's next turn, that is, when your pawn finds itself yet again in danger, and no one is there to save it. You have now effectively sacrificed your queen for nothing, and have essentially sent the rest of your game into chaos. Do you see why this is bad?"

"Yes," Flynn answered, "But why are you telling me this?"

Bi smiled knowingly. "Someday you will understand." She slipped the pawn back into her pocket. "For now, get some rest. These next few days are not going to be easy."

Noise. Noise is everywhere. It fills the boy's ears. Gunshots, yelling, footsteps pounding up the stairs.

The young boy runs upstairs to where his parents should be. They are out in the hallway, looking around, their eyes full of worry. His father takes the boy's hand and the three of them run together, arriving at the end of the hallway, where the stairs go up to the roof.

The door at the opposite end of the hallway behind them explodes, and soldiers flood into the hall, their black armor and silver parts shining, guns raised.

"Go," the father says, and he pushes the mother and son up the stairs. The son looks back to see his father battling the soldiers. Despite his military skill, he does not last very long. He falls to the ground.

The mother leads the boy up the stairs quickly, opening the metal door that leads to the roof before locking it behind them. She runs to the north end, where the ladder is. She peers over the side before stumbling back suddenly. She backs away from the edge quickly, going to the opposite side of the roof before collapsing. The boy runs to her. She has a bullet wound in her head.

"You cannot escape down the ladder," she tells him. "There are more waiting at the bottom." Her eyes start to glaze over. "I love you Flynn. You will grow to be a good man. Get into grandpa's office, ok?"

The twelve year old boy looks into his mother's eyes. "But Poppy is dead."

"I know, I know," his mother says. She grabs his arm. Her breaths are ragged. "But you can still live." She blinks multiple times and suddenly her eyes become fully clear, and her voice changes. It sounds eerie and drawn out. "There will be a time when you will be bent to your full potential, Flynn. You will have to make the right decision or everything you love will be lost. The Firestorm approaches, Flynn. The trial of a lifetime is at hand." She closes her eyes.

"Mom?" The boy grabs her hand. "Mom, the men are coming, you can't be here right now. We need to get off of the roof."

The boy hears banging on the door and his eyes grow wide. He backs toward the edge of the building, looking down to the ground three stories below. Beneath him is a decorative metal ledge above the window to his grandfather's office. Slowly, he backs over the edge, quickly grabbing part of the metal ornament and swinging himself through the window, shattering the glass as the soldiers break down the door and flood onto the roof.

The boy, now in his grandfather's office, reaches out with his hands, using his mind to lift a heavy bookshelf off of one wall and placing it in front of the door. The energy drains him but even the strongest man couldn't move it. What the boy doesn't realize is that these aren't men.

Some of the robotic soldiers come back down the stairs, and start pushing at the door. The boy is surprised when the bookshelf starts moving, inching out of the way as the barrage continues.

Looking around frantically, he sees the two closest things to weapons he can find. The mataka and hiveblade, two ancient Chinese weapons that his grandfather had found years ago before he died.

The boy uses his powers again to bend and shatter the glass of the case they are held in. He then pulls the objects to him, letting them fly across the room and into his grasp. He goes into the corner of the room and crouches down, blocking his small body with the shield as soldiers begin shooting bullets through the bookshelf. To the boy's surprise, the mataka actually stops them.

The boy hears a noise and looks up to see a soldier climbing through the window. He raises his shield, but he cannot cover himself from the bullets coming from the bookshelf and this new threat at the same time. The soldier above him raises his gun as the boy closes his eyes and a shot rings out.

The soldier falls off of the windowsill and the boy looks up, surprised to be alive. He sees another figure come into view on the windowsill.

A person. A *human* person

“Hey there young man,” she says. “Looks like you need some help.” She reaches her hand out to him, and he takes it. “My name is Bi. Welcome to the IPA.”

Flynn woke up with his body covered in sweat. He hopped out of bed, standing up and taking deep breaths with his eyes closed.

Flynn had seen this dream many times. The night of his parent’s deaths. The night he joined the IPA. Nearly three years ago.

He had never understood what his mother had said about the "Firestorm." Questions constantly crowded his mind. What was it? When would it happen? What would happen if he failed? The whole occurrence was odd, and he had nowhere to go to find answers.

After cooling off, Flynn got back into the bed and pulled the sheets up, listening to the soft hum of the Rizen, which was flying somewhere above the United States. The noise calmed him, and he tried to go back to sleep.

He closed his eyes, and the vision of the dream filled his mind. The same dream, every night. For the past three years.

7- Werewolf Effect

The Heights, Just Outside of Manhattan
New York, U.S.A
12:00 a.m.
Flynn

Flynn ran down the dark, damp road, the starry sky reflecting off of the Hudson River beneath the city skyline ahead. He could hear the heavy breathing of his squad members behind him. Flynn had always been the fastest in the group.

They turned a corner and continued running. They had parked the Rizen in an ally's garage in New Jersey, someone that Bi had claimed was a member of an underground group called the Red Army, and were now heading to the rendezvous where they would meet up with a squad from Clan Pris.

Clan Pris had been struggling in the war for some time now, but they had never asked for help. They said it was because none of the soldiers from other clans had the correct expertise that was needed, but some people believed that it was just because Captain Pris didn't want to ask for help because it showed weakness. Flynn didn't know what to believe.

The squad came around another corner and slowed as they saw a group of soldiers standing in front of a dock that was lined with boats of many sizes, bobbing up and down in the water of the Hudson.

The soldiers looked much like the ones from Flynn's squad, but their black suits had purple highlights instead of Vilo's red, and all of them were snipers, which he could see based on the shape of their helmets, and a small insignia that was on the shoulder piece of their armor. Flynn himself has a different insignia, which marked him as point, or the forward leader of the squad.

Bi walked forward and approached the sergeant from the other squad, whose ranking was made obvious by the insignia welded onto her suit's shoulder. Her suit also differed from the others with spikes on the shoulders and two small, wing-like pieces of metal protruding upward on either side of her helmet.

"Squad Sergeant Andromeda," Bi said, and they shook hands. "It is a pleasure to meet you at last."

"The same to you, Sergeant Bi," Andromeda said. "I have heard quite a bit about you. They told me you were the best intellect outside of Clan Troy. Due to our war's condition, I hope they are right." She turned to the rest of Bi's squad. "We have three boats. My squad will take two small ones. Your squad, along with me, will take the largest boat. They await us at the end of the dock. There are Enforcement patrol boats that go along the river. Here in the upper bay is the safest way to get across. We must leave now if we are going to sneak past them."

Both groups began making their way down the dock. The soldiers from Pris got to their boats first. They all seemed to be sizing up Blackeye, although Flynn couldn't tell if it was because she was the only sniper in his group and therefore could be competition, or if they were checking her out because she was a girl.

As the soldiers began getting onto the boat, one of them turned toward her. "Hey, these are some pretty high buildings we're going to be shooting off of. Are you sure you're going to be able to handle it?"

Blackeye walked past them confidently, seeming not to have noticed. The soldier turned to his comrade and shrugged before pulling himself up the ladder and onto the boat. Flynn chuckled and continued walking.

He was surprised by how big the boat was. It was a multiple-story yacht, complete with an outdoor barbeque deck, a hot tub, and the name *Tiara* printed in gold letters on the side.

"It would be a shame to put this nice of a boat to waste," Zane said.

Ryan turned to him. "Maybe we can ask to take it home after we leave."

Zane chuckled. "Well, we need to survive this war in order to leave."

"And we need to get on the boat to help in the war," Bi called down to them from the deck. "Stop wasting time and get on."

Flynn got in after the twins, leaving Tarff to get on last. He rocked the entire boat as he climbed up the ladder and plopped down on a couch near the back of the boat, setting down the massive backpack of the group's equipment he had brought next to him.

Flynn looked over to see Bi put a small rock that she had picked up on the dock into a pouch on her suits' utility belt. He was about to ask why she had acquired such a pointless object but he decided against it. Bi had always explained to him that sometimes her abilities would randomly inspire her to do things that could benefit her in the future. It was always interesting for him to see what she would use these things for later.

His eye then turned to Andromeda as she strode to the helm and began to pull away from the dock. The other boats followed.

"They've built a lot of upgrades into this," Zane said. "A carbon fiber frame reinforced with dragon steel webbing. This boat came straight from Clan Xion."

Flynn looked out over the river at the city skyline. New York had been abandoned years ago due to the war. The battles of Clan Pris here were crucial to the IPA winning the war. Without it, Cadmore industries would have a great upper hand. Controlling New York meant controlling the war.

Flynn had only seen Manhattan in pictures. Now, being here, especially in a time of war, he began to worry even more about how far he was from Emily. If something bad happened to her while he was gone...

Flynn pushed the thought out of his mind, not letting it distract him. He walked away from Zane and Ryan, who were still admiring the boat's structure, and went over to Cago, who was sitting on a cushioned bench. He was pressing a button on his belt, turning his suit on and off, watching as it spread out over his body, and then ripple back into the box.

"Do you really think something that can fit inside of this tiny box will protect me from Enforcement?" Cago asked as he approached.

"I have seen it work many wonders before," Flynn said. "This is the best armor that you can find anywhere."

Cago sighed. "I guess I'll just have to learn to trust it."

"Yeah," Flynn agreed. "It takes a while to get used to."

Flynn heard a noise at the back of the boat and turned toward it. Five shiny black patrol boats were in the water behind them.

"Blast!" Andromeda said. "They knew we were coming." She flipped some switches on the boat's dashboard and the boat exited stealth mode, allowing them to pick up speed. The other boats followed suit.

Andromeda looked forward and then turned to Bi. "They have boats waiting at our dock. There is one more we could go to and still be safe. It is about a half mile southeast of us, around the bend." She pointed to the alleged dock, which was out of sight due to the buildings. "Should we try it?"

Bi paused for a moment before nodding.

Andromeda picked up a small, box-like commlink microphone from the dashboard. "Boats two and three, change course. We are going to Port Gravesend."

Flynn and Cago watched intently out of the back of the boat as they all changed course, turning to go farther down river at a diagonal instead of cutting straight across it to the city.

Andromeda stepped down from the helm and went to the back of the boat. She seemed to be searching the water with some type of scanner built into her helmet. She cursed.

"What's wrong?" Bi asked.

"They have an intercessor." Andromeda said.

Flynn remembered that intercessor boats were very strong and very fast. They typically had a heavily armored front allowing them to speed forward into battle before blowing themselves up next to an enemy boat. Meaning they needed to destroy it before it got close.

"The only way to destroy it is to take out the driving programming system but hitting it will be difficult. That thing will be onto us in seconds if we don't take it out. I'll get my best sniper." She began talking to one of her squad members from another boat. "Redshift, we have an intercessor in coordinates 5.8.9. It's a-"

She got cut off by the sound of an explosion and they all watched as a ball of flame erupted from the water a few hundred yards behind the boat, leaving the interceptor in pieces.

The eyes of the soldiers on the boat drifted to Blackeye, who was kneeling on one of the front-facing benches, her sniper rifle pointed out to the water behind them. She pulled it up and slung it back over her shoulder.

Andromeda cleared her throat uncomfortably. "Nice shot." She went back to the helm.

Flynn turned on the thermal scanner inside of his helmet, and he began studying the boats' positions. There were five of them, spread out in a fan about 800 yards away, but they were slowly catching up. The dock was still out of view around the bend of the river.

"Do you think we will be able to make it to the dock?" Flynn asked Bi.

"If not, we will have to fight," Bi said. "And if we fight, we had better hope for good luck."

After a few minutes, the boats started attacking. They were ranged attacks, and they missed frequently, but occasionally they landed a hit, making the whole boat shudder. Some of the snipers began firing back at the boats, but they had much more armor than the intercessor, and no weak spots.

Flynn pulled out his gun. He had been training with it for a while. It had decent power, and shot three bullets in rapid succession, penetrating through an enemy's armor easily.

Kneeling, with the back of the bench blocking him from the incoming bullets, Flynn raised his gun toward the boats in the water and began shooting. After a while, he found that hitting the boat itself, although easier, was ineffective. It was better to try to hit the soldiers on the deck to reduce the amount of damage being taken.

Flynn heard a whirring noise behind him and he turned around. In the middle of the boat, on a pedestal that had been raised from below deck, was a full-sized turret. Sitting on top of it was Zane.

Zane smiled. "I like this boat." He then began firing at the enemies, every hit resounding across the open water and every miss sending a splash of mist into the air.

Even with all three of the boat's soldiers engaged in the fight, and with the help of the turret, they only managed to take out one boat before the others were nearly onto them and were loading up their own powerful guns.

"Bad news," Andromeda said. "The farthest-back boat has a railgun. Once that cannon charges up, it will only take three shots for them to kill us all. Concentrate your fire on it."

This time, not even Blackeye could destroy it. The front three boats created a barricade for their comrade, and the railgun that they were setting up was far too heavily armored. They had to do something else.

"Zane," Flynn yelled over all the noise of the fighting. "Can you jam their turret's targeting system?"

He shook his head, "I already tried. I just don't have that kind of equipment with me. The stuff that I have isn't advanced enough. I already tried."

Flynn looked back to the boat. They were almost ready. "If we can somehow make it so they can't hit us..." Flynn mumbled to himself. He watched as the soldiers on the other two Clan Pris boats tried frantically to take down the cannon, and suddenly a thought occurred to him. "Cago! When you were in the car after your aunt's funeral, didn't you make some kind of dark cloud that affected the robot's vision and thermal scanners?"

"Yes but-"

“Cago, you need to use your powers,” Flynn said, “If they don’t know where to aim then they won’t hit us.”

“I just-” Cago’s eyes darted between Flynn and the other boats. Why was he hesitating? “I don’t know if I can cover all this space without a power overload.”

“Can’t you just put it around them?” Flynn asked.

“I-I don’t know how to do that!” Cago stuttered.

Flynn thought for a moment. Power overloads could be dangerous. If an Ironborn used too much power, any number of things could happen. “We’ll die otherwise.” He looked back at the Enforcement boat, whose cannon was almost finished charging up. “We only have a few seconds. You need to do it now!”

Cago hesitated, not knowing what to do.

“Cago!” Flynn cried.

Cago reached his hands into the air, and a dark mist surrounded them. The boats behind them and all the buildings disappeared as the mist spread out to cover every boat on the river. Flynn could only see a few feet around him. Cago disengaged his helmet and took in deep breaths of air.

“Hey, are you ok?” Flynn looked over at him as he struggled to stand up. “Cago what-”

He watched as Cago's eyes rolled back into his head and gave Flynn an eerie smile before suddenly disappearing into the black mist.

"Oh sh-" Flynn got slammed into by an unseen force, and knocked back across the floor of the boat. Staggering, he got to his feet.

Flynn ran up toward where the helm should be but got knocked over again by the invisible force. He turned and punched the creature, and for a second Cago flashed back into view, crouching a few feet away from him. The darkened form of him snarled and leapt through the air, becoming invisible again.

Flynn rolled out of the way and began talking rapidly into his helmet comm. "Bi, we have a problem. Something happened to Cago and now he is attacking me. I am afraid that if-" Flynn was cut off as the boat began rocking back and forth, slamming into the water and jostling sharply. Cago had made it to the helm.

Flynn stood up and walked unsteadily toward the front of the boat, using a railing so he wouldn't fall over. Listening intently, he managed to shoot half-blindly into the mist at where he could see a small hazy shadow of Cago's form. The gun, of course, did no damage to his suit, but it got the creature's attention.

The darkened form of Cago hissed and leapt nearly ten feet over a railing to the place where Flynn was, catching him off guard. Its speed surprised Flynn, and he got knocked over before he could get back up, the gun flying from his hands.

The creature began wrestling with Flynn, and surprisingly, was winning. Based on physical build and fighting experience, Flynn should have easily beaten Cago. Apparently this darkness gave him strength.

Flynn watched another figure leap out of the mist and slam into Cago, pinning him to the ground. The darkness might make him stronger, but not as strong as Tarff.

Cago struggled on the deck of the boat as the forms Bi and Andromeda approached him from out of the dark mist. Flynn stood up and walked over.

Bi placed a hand on Cago's forehead as he tried to escape Tarff's grasp. "Leave us," Bi said to him.

Cago suddenly went limp, passing out. Tarff carried him over to lay him down on a bench.

"What on earth was that?" Flynn asked, exasperated.

"It's a kind of werewolf effect," Bi said. "Instead of the physical and mental pain that the two of you get after an overload," she said to Flynn and Tarff, "sometimes people go crazy after using their powers too much. They go crazy and then can't think clearly. I've seen it before, but it wasn't anything like this." She paused. "I'll have to talk to him about it once he wakes back up."

“We are nearing the dock,” Andromeda said, walking up behind them. “We’ve gone around the peninsula. We are getting close to safety.”

As she said those words, the three boats exited the mist of darkness, and Flynn nearly choked at what he saw. Not two hundred yards away, towering high into the sky, was a military-grade Cadmore Industries battleship.

8- Whale Shark

The Hudson River, Manhattan
New York, USA
12:30 a.m.
Flynn

Looking up at the massive boat, Flynn felt like an insect. White letters on the side of the boat spelled the words *Whale Shark*, and four gigantic cannons sat atop the boat's deck, along with many others that were smaller.

"What do we do?" Flynn asked Bi.

Bi stood on the deck with her arms folded, surveying the situation. "That is an A12 class battleship. If it hasn't found us already, it won't take them long to do so." She pressed a button on her wrist. "Blackeye, what's it looking like up there?"

Blackeye's comm was specifically set to transmit to the inside of Bi's helmet, so only she could hear the information Blackeye relayed to her as she scanned the deck with the scope on her sniper rifle.

"Hmm..." Bi said, appearing to be speaking to no one, "Have they spotted us?" Bi waited a moment before turning to the other sergeant. "Andromeda, can we get to the shore?"

"Not without getting destroyed by those cannons," Andromeda gestured to the massive boat above them.

Bi considered this for a moment. "Go straight towards the battleship, and order the others to do the same."

"What?" Andromeda asked, astonished.

Bi turned towards her. "The *Whale Shark* has a blind spot on the portside of the boat. We can't destroy the ship, but if we can get one of the smaller patrol boats there, we might be able to sneak onboard. From there, Zane may be able to shut down the boat's targeting momentarily, possibly long enough for us to get away without getting blown out of the water." She looked up to where the massive dual-barrelled cannons were currently hidden from view.

"And what will the rest of us be doing?" Andromeda asked.

"According to our scanners the patrol boats have turned back to get reinforcements," Bi said. "You'll be making sure they won't become a problem if they come back."

"That might get dicey but I think we can do it," Andromeda said, looking out to the water behind them. "Let's hope that you can be fast enough that our assistance is not needed."

"Zane, are you ready to blow something up?" Bi said through her comm.

Flynn heard the response from the inside of his helmet. "It would be my pleasure."

Zane placed another hand on the side of the boat, enjoying the feeling of his suit magnetically gripping onto the metal. Zane had helped design the suits himself, and he felt secure using them to their limits.

Looking down, he could see Bi, Flynn, Ryan and Blackeye climbing up behind him, the black water churning softly hundreds of feet below. Tarff had agreed to stay behind and watch Cago. The two of them were standing on one of the smaller Clan Pris boats which they had quickly switched too before sneakily maneuvering it up next to the battleship, leaving the larger boat out on the water as a distraction. No patrols had managed to spot them yet, but they would be well within view soon.

Looking up, Zane heard a noise. It sounded like some mechanical system on the boat had engaged, but Zane could not yet see what it was. His question was answered quickly.

Four massive booms shook the boat as the cannons fired down at the boats below. "Andromeda!" Bi said into her comm. "They've found you!"

Looking down at the small boat beneath them, Zane felt like it couldn't stand a chance against the massive guns. At least it was too close to the boat to be in range. For now.

At long last, Zane reached the top of the boat and peered over the edge. Enforcement troops patrolled the deck, surveying the ocean with their scanners. They looked menacing with their shiny black helmets, armored skeleton, and powerful guns. Although there were plenty of troops, no one had to man the ship's cannons. The boat itself was a robot.

"What's our plan?" Zane asked as Bi came up beside him.

"We outsmart the officers."

Outsmarting the officer was a breakthrough that Bi had found nearly a year ago. There is one commander in each legion of Enforcement troops. For years, the IPA believed that they had better programming, allowing them to have better tactics than a normal soldier or specialist. Sergeant Bi however, had realized that they had the same programming, but they were also connected to a satellite that transferred information to the Enforcement headquarters. The bot would perform to the best of its abilities, but when it came in contact with a problem that its programming could not solve, it would send the message to a human Enforcement officer. So outsmarting the legion commander was not hard. What you needed to do was outsmart the human officer.

“Watch the patrols,” Bi said. “They have a pattern.”

Zane watched. Every few minutes, a patrol would pass by, occasionally stopping and searching the water before moving on. “The primary scanning tower should be in the stern of the ship,” Zane said.

“I see it,” Ryan said. “My helmet's sensors are picking up major radio transmissions coming from the tower above it.”

“Perfect,” Bi said. “Our charges should be able to blow it up. Hopefully we can get away before they transfer over to the secondary scanners.” Bi paused as some troops walked by, their metal feet clanking against the deck of the boat. “Zane and Flynn, you set the charges for the tower. Ryan and Blackeye, you set up the transmitter. I will go and see if I can confuse the bots to buy us some more time.”

Bi waited until the next patrol passed. “Let's move.”

Everyone vaulted the railing, trying to be as quiet as possible.

Zane ran silently across the dull metal deck, Flynn following close behind. At this point in the mission, stealth was their greatest objective. Zane guessed that later they would probably have to fight but for now it was best to not be seen.

Pulling out some of his tools, Zane quietly decoded the lock to a door and pulled it open to reveal an empty hallway in front of them. Zane ran down the hall and turned a corner to find two soldiers facing away from them. He backpedaled and signaled for Flynn to stop. Flynn nodded, understanding the situation.

As they waited behind the wall for the soldiers to pass, Zane heard a low rumbling noise that sounded like an explosion somewhere on the boat.

Zane waited for a second before looking around the corner again to see that the patrol had moved on. Starting slowly, he began to run down the hall, speeding up as he went. He was surprised at how quietly Flynn could run. Zane couldn't even tell he was there.

When he turned the next corner, he was shocked as gunshots filled the space in front of him. He quickly took cover behind a wall beyond the door.

Peeking around the corner, Zane could see two soldiers guarding the door to the communications room. One soldier began advancing towards where Zane was hidden. Zane looked back toward where he had come from and saw that Flynn had not yet crossed in front of the hall where the door was located.

"Two guards. D-80 class," Zane said into his hemet. "One is coming towards me."

Flynn nodded and drew his Hiveblade. As the soldier advanced past the corner, gun raised towards Zane, Flynn leapt forwards, his blade penetrating the bot's armor, its cords sparking as it collapsed to the ground. As the other guard at the door began firing at Flynn, he spun his staff, deflecting each bullet as it came his way. Flynn had done a lot of training to be able to do that.

Drawing his gun, Zane stepped out from behind the wall and opened fire. The soldier dropped to one knee as a blast struck his leg.

Seizing the opportunity, Flynn reached forwards and closed his fist, using his powers. Flynn extended his staff as the bot fell towards him, dispatching the soldier as it was impaled by the tip of Flynn's weapon.

By now, the computer must have noticed that the bots had not sent in an all-clear signal in longer than their scheduled time.

"Everyone," Zane said into his helmet, "They know we're here."

They ran forwards to the door and Zane decoded this panel as he had the first. The door then slid open automatically as he punched in the code.

Flynn swiftly dispatched the soldier that manned the inside of the room. Zane ran over to the screen monitors that spanned the walls of the circular space. He pulled three rectangular boxes from his suit's utility belt, engaging the explosives as he placed them periodically around the control center.

"Charges set," he said into his comm.

"Ready?" Flynn asked.

Zane nodded. "Let's move."

Ryan hung from the side of the battleship, one hand on a cable attached to the railing, the other holding the receiver. "Are you sure this is safe?" he called up to Blackeye, who was guarding him from the deck. She glared down at him in response.

"Whatever you say." He let go of the cable, letting his harness hold him up. He began welding the receiver onto the side of the boat's hull. The receiver's job was to get the transmission from the fob that set off the explosive charges. If he didn't get the receiver set up, there was no chance that anything would blow up.

Ryan was halfway done when a message came through the speakers inside his helmet. "Everyone, they know we're here."

Ryan quickened his pace. "Get ready, Blackeye."

He heard footsteps on the deck and watched Blackeye draw her sniper rifle, crouching behind a pile of crates. He watched as she silently aimed and fired, dropping soldier after soldier.

She may not be nice but at least she's good at what she does. Ryan thought as he finished and began climbing the cable, easily scaling the twenty feet to the deck, given his suit's added strength.

When he reached the deck, he dove over next to Blackeye and began firing his gun. He was half as effective as she was but at least it helped.

Ryan heard footsteps behind him and saw Zane and Flynn running towards them, dodging fire from Enforcement.

They reached the crates and took cover, breathing heavily. With Flynn and Zane's added help, they had a chance at holding off their enemy forces, but they were still surrounded and could only last so long. They were sitting ducks.

"Come on Bi," Zane whispered. "Where are you?"

Talia crept along the edge of a wall, moving towards the massive cannons. She was worried for the others in her squad but knew that they were capable of taking care of themselves.

Where the wall ended, she could see the massive quad-cannon nearly thirty yards in front of her, blocked by an open deck swarming with soldiers.

She reached down to her belt and pulled out a rectangular explosive. She then activated it as it magnetized itself to the wall.

Taking three steps back, she threw the small rock she had picked up on the dock, and ran behind some crates. Peeking through a hole between the crates, Bi could see a group of soldiers inspecting the stone, which had landed right next to where she had placed the explosive. She quickly pulled out the explosive's detonator and pressed the button on top.

The explosion rumbled the hull of the boat, but didn't do very much damage. At least it drew the rest of the soldiers away from the cannons.

Coming out from behind the crates, but still in the cover of the smoke from the explosion, Bi sprinted to the railing and vaulted over, pulling herself onto the side of the battleship. From there, she crawled forwards, using her suit to allow her to magnetize to the metal and move towards the bow of the boat.

When she neared the cannons, she vaulted back over the railing and sprinted to the base of the giant machine. Staying in the shadows, she placed her charges around the base, trying specifically to disable the movement of the cannon, not destroy it. Destroying it would not be possible with the amount of explosives she had, but disabling its movement could buy them more time.

After setting up the charges, she sprinted back to the railing and once again climbed onto the side of the boat. After traveling far from the cannons, she set off the charges.

She heard a big explosion, but could not see anything. Having no time to lose, she continued climbing towards the stern. After getting nearly above where the boat was hidden in the water, she looked up and saw that there were Enforcement soldiers battling against what appeared to be an enemy hidden behind a pile of crates.

"Back in trouble again." Smiling and shaking her head, she threw a grenade onto the deck and ducked as flames flew out in all directions.

Vaulting back over the railing, she ran to the crates and dove behind them as her squad continued to battle the force on the other side of them.

"Took you long enough," Zane said.

Down at the speed boat, Tarff looked up at the small black dots climbing down the side of the battleship. He had heard multiple explosions and had seen plenty of gun fire, but everyone appeared to be alright.

Finally, the squad reached the ship.

Zane pulled out a detonator from his belt. "Here goes nothing." He pressed the button and the large ship shook as a volley of waves rocked the speed boat. Smoke rose from the stern of the battleship.

"The scanners should be disabled now," Bi told Andromeda, "Let's go before they can get a secondary system online."

Andromeda punched the gas, and they sped away towards the shore.

"I disabled the main cannons," Bi said. "Just in case they tried to fire manually without the system."

"So that's what you were doing that whole time?" Ryan asked.

"What did the rest of you do?" Tarff asked.

"I went to the control room with Flynn," Zane said. "We came in contact with some soldiers, but took them down without too much trouble."

"Meanwhile," Ryan cut in, "I was hanging from the side of the boat welding the receiver in while I was being attacked by Enforcement bots."

"Which I saved him from after I set up the explosives that saved our lives," Zane added

"Saved our lives?" Ryan said. "More like ran for *your* life and putting us in more trouble than we were in before. And, for the record, your 'explosives' wouldn't have worked without the receiver that I put in."

"Well," Zane said, "I bet I killed more enemies than you."

Ryan laughed. "I got thirty-five."

Zane folded his arms. "Forty-one."

"No way," Ryan complained, pulling five dollars from his belt. "You don't even train that much."

"My skill comes from birth," Zane bragged, taking the money from him. Another bet won.

"Yeah, right," Ryan said. "I was at your birth and it was pathetic."

"You had only been born for twenty seconds," Zane complained. "There's no way you remember it."

"It was three minutes," Ryan corrected.

"Besides," Zane pointed out, "maybe that's why I'm better at fighting. Maybe whoever chose to put me second felt bad for me."

"Whatever," Ryan said.

The speed boat was nearing the shore when the other boats from Clan Pris caught up.

"Get ready," Andromeda said. "We're coming in fast."

As they came up to a small wooden dock, Andromeda expertly maneuvered next to it and everyone piled out. The other two boats came in as well and everyone ran down the boardwalk onto the sandy beach.

Tarff heard a low mechanical noise behind him as they ran up into an abandoned parking lot. Turning, he watched as the massive cannons on the battleship, which had now rebooted, turned towards the shore and fired, blowing the boats into oblivion.

9-Plans

Arguan Tower, Manhattan
New York, USA
2:30 am
Flynn

"I see you made it in one piece," Commander Sjen stood before Flynn and the others. After leaving the beach, they had used underground tunnels to reach the main Clan Pris headquarters, which was located in a large building near the middle of the island city.

"Thanks to Sergeant Bi, yes," Andromeda said. "We ran into a few..." She paused, glancing over at Cago. He was now back to his normal self, his head bowed in shame. "Unseen difficulties, but we were able to make it back with minimal injuries."

"Good." Sjen's voice was definitely Asian, and he appeared to be nearly seven feet tall, although Flynn knew that the IPA's suits could alter the look of someone's body and the sound of their voice. "We can't afford to lose anyone else. We got word that two juggernauts are being sent to aid Enforcement here in New York."

"Two!" Andromeda exclaimed. "What will they throw at us next? The Blood Squad?"

Sjen chuckled. "Hopefully not."

Flynn had only heard of the Blood Squad in stories before. The five members were the most elite robots in the Cadmore Industries military, and none had been seen to take a single bit of damage from battle. David Cadmore himself had built them as his personal guard and luckily they hadn't been able to be replicated by Dr. Griffin after his death. Clan Troy had been fighting against them since the war began. If Troy couldn't kill them then Pris wouldn't stand a chance. Luckily, they weren't their imminent problem.

The square office that the group was standing in had windows on two sides with a whiteboard and a map on the other two walls. It seemed to have been a large business building before the war began. Sjen turned and motioned to the map. "I've heard that Squad Sergeant Bi has a reputation for… interesting but effective battle tactics, which might be exactly what we need here. Do you have any insight on how we might gain advantage over our enemies?"

Bi paused for a moment. "I would need to further study the enemies' previous tactics and battle positions. Do you mind if I use some of your battle recordings?"

Sjen motioned to a soldier to his right. "Minor can show you to our file room." He turned to face the rest of the group. "The rest of you are excused. I would like to speak with Andromeda alone."

As the group shuffled out of the room and followed a Clan Pris soldier down the hallway, Bi fell into step next to Flynn. “I want you to speak with Cago and figure out what happened. I want to make sure it won't happen again.”

“Yes sergeant.” Flynn watched Bi walk ahead and split off from the group, following Minor until they both passed out of sight around a corner.

The soldier led them a long way before stopping at a hallway. “These are your bunk rooms on the left. We will notify you when we need your assistance. If you have any questions, just call for me. My name is Nebula. Sjen will know where to find me.”

She turned to leave as Flynn’s group chose rooms. It was obvious who would go with each other. Zane and Ryan were brothers, Bi and Blackeye were the only girls, and Tarff practically took up an entire room by himself so he had to be alone.

Which left Flynn with Cago. Perfect.

The bunk rooms were decently sized, with one bunk bed on the right side of the room and two dressers on the other. Flynn and Cago, of course, had all of their belongings in just a simple backpack, so they set them on the ground.

Closing the door, Flynn disengaged his suit. The suits were comfortable, but Flynn much preferred the T-shirt and shorts he wore underneath. Cago followed Flynn’s lead with his own suit before laying down on the bottom bunk so Flynn took the top. They both rested for a moment, glad for the comfort of a bed.

Peering down, Flynn tried to study Cago's body language like Bi had taught him to over the past few years. His eyes were closed a little too tightly, as if he was trying to concentrate on something, and his body was tense, showing signs of anxiety. Flynn leaned back onto his mattress, thinking.

"Thanks for saving me," Cago said from the bed below him. "I shouldn't have used my powers."

Flynn paused before responding. "You saved our lives by doing so. It was my fault, I pushed you to use your abilities, without thinking of alternate consequences. There were other-"

"Don't blame yourself," Cago interrupted. "I've known about this for years. I don't even remember what happens when I go dark. One moment I'm on the boat, the next I'm tied up and being slung over Tarff's shoulder in the hallway of an office building."

"So it's not a form of you then?" Flynn asked.

"I don't exactly know," Cago replied. "I've heard it talk to me before, urging me to use my powers more and more until I have no more control left. In fact, with the amount of power I used, I'm surprised that you could stop it."

Flynn chuckled. "It wasn't easy."

Cago paused for a moment. "Well it's been less than forty-eight hours and my new family already knows both my biggest secrets. I think that's a new record."

They both laughed lightly. Suddenly, there was a knock on their door. Flynn reengaged his suit, motioning for Cago to do the same. Flynn had been told it was best never to show your face in the IPA outside of your squad. You never knew when information might leak and Enforcement would find out who you really are.

"Come in," Flynn said.

It was Nebula. "Sorry for the intrusion, but Sjen would like to speak with your squad."

Flynn hopped down from his bunk and followed Nebula as she left the room, Cago trailing behind.

They quickly gathered the others from their rooms and headed down the hall. After lots of turns and a few flights of stairs, Nebula led them into a large library.

Bi, Minor, Andromeda and Sjen were standing around a circular table that had a holographic projection of a sector of New York City. They were all deep in conversation when the group arrived.

"...left flank with the ironbots," Bi was saying, "drawing them closer to this side."

"Unless they take the hard way to deplete our forces," Andromeda stated.

"Then we give them a reason not to," Bi continued. "Last time your forces defeated the juggernaut by crushing it with a garbage truck from the top of the YMO building. You already stated that that probably wouldn't work again because they would suspect it, but if they know that it's coming, the juggernaut will surely move out of the way, leading it right to where we want it. It is a checkmate position. The juggernaut will die either way."

"That might actually work," Sjen said. It was weird hearing him agree with someone. It didn't match the way he typically spoke. "Although your trap won't be strong enough to destroy it."

"That's where they come in," Bi pointed to her squad huddled around Nebula.

Sjen chuckled. "You really think that you can take out a juggernaut with less than ten soldiers? I didn't know you were from Clan Troy."

Flynn bit his tongue before he said something. Clan Troy was the most elite group of soldiers in the IPA. The best units from other clans were pulled into it and doubly trained. They were the Iron Warrior's personal guard, and were currently fighting in the war in Florida. The rest of the IPA had assumed their abilities were mostly just talk until Captain Dax himself went to aid him and got nearly half of one of his dens killed in one day on the same battle field that Clan Troy had never lost a single soldier on.

Nearly everyone admired them and they really were an unbeatable force, but Bi's squadron had always held a grudge against them because even after years of asking, they had never let Bi in to help them with their second biggest problem, Project Redstone, which was finding the Cadmore Industries headquarters. Everyone in the squad agreed that, with the resources that Clan Troy's research team had, it would probably take less than a week for Bi to figure out where it was but, for some reason, they had never even considered her offers. Mentions of Clan Troy were always tentious in their squad. Troy was good at what they did, but everyone had unshared and mixed feelings toward them. Deep down, Flynn hoped this mission might make them think about letting her join.

"They aren't from Clan Troy, but they still have skill, and I happen to have a plan," Bi said. "One that I am confident my soldiers are capable of pulling off."

"I'm aware that you have a plan," Sjen sighed. "Let's just hope you're right."

10- A Hero's Send Off

A Stinky Sewer Drain, Manhattan
New York, USA
10:00 a.m.
Flynn

Flynn took a deep breath, trying hard not to get worried about his current situation. After Bi had explained her genius but dangerous plan, Flynn had gone straight to his assigned post. It was in a small chamber that made up an intersection of sewage drain pipes, which happened to be right beneath the enemy. Flynn could hear their marching from above him, along with the electric sounds of their plasma guns firing off.

"Scorpius on standby," he said into his comm. He always used the nickname Ryan had given him on missions. It was tradition.

"Affirmative." The altered voice of Zane came through his helmet. Zane was copying Flynn's lateral position, but was in a separate tunnel about one hundred yards away. "Waiting for command."

"Excellent," Bi told them both. "I'll give you the signal soon. Start setting up the explosives."

Flynn pulled the charges off of his belt and placed them around the tunnel.

"Scorpius, there is a patrol coming your way," Bi said.

Flynn frantically gathered up the explosives, detaching them from the walls as quickly as he could so that the soldiers would not see them when they entered the space. He could now hear the patrol getting closer, their footsteps echoing through the tunnel to his left. As he went to get the last explosive, he saw the patrol down the tunnel. He quickly dove to one side of the room and held perfectly still. He then reached down and pressed a button on his wrist, activating his suit's cloaking mode.

As far as the IPA knew, the suits could make you invisible to Cadmore Industry's sensors and scanners so long as you didn't move, but Flynn still wasn't completely confident in their ability.

He held his breath as two patrol soldiers walked into the intersection, their metal feet sloshing through the low water. They paused and slowly glanced around the room, looking directly at where he was sitting, trying to stay as silent as possible. Then, to Flynn's relief, they moved on. Flynn waited a while after they disappeared out of sight to set up the explosives again.

"Scorpius on stand by," Flynn said.

"Good," Bi said through the comms. "Blackeye, do you have your mark?"

Flynn didn't need to hear the answer to know what it was. Blackeye always had her mark. She could snipe an Enforcement soldier from a mile away in her sleep.

"Alright," a high, raspy voice came through. It took Flynn a second to realize it was Cago speaking through the voice scrambler. He wasn't quite used to Cago's coded voice yet, unlike the others who he had been hearing for years. "I'm in position."

"You say 'Cago on stand by,'" Ryan said through the comm.

"Give him a break Ryan," Zane said. "This is his first mission."

"That is why I'm teaching him protocol," Ryan said back.

"Well-"

"I'm fine," Cago cut in. "Cago on stand by."

"Alright," Bi said. "Move toward second positions."

As Flynn ran down the tunnel that the Enforcement patrol had come from, he thought it interesting that Bi had not said anything to either Cago or the twins. Flynn tried to think of why she hadn't. Maybe there was no reason. *No,* he thought, *Bi always has a reason.*

Turning around a bend in the tunnel, Flynn turned on his comm. "Scorpius on standby for target two." Zane and Cago said the same for their own positions.

"On my mark, set off the charges," Bi said. "Ready..." She paused. "Now!"

Flynn heard a series of explosions as he and the others blew up the bombs.

"Move into position three," Bi ordered.

Flynn began running back towards where he had come from. As the intersection came into view, he ducked down and rebooted his cloaking device.

Ahead of him, in his intersection, was a massive, twenty foot tall Enforcement soldier. A juggernaut. It was barely wide enough to fit in the New York main sewage pipes, which could comfortably fit three cars across and double that many up.

Just as planned, the explosives had blown a hole through the ceiling of the intersection, causing the street above to cave in and the juggernaut to fall through to the tunnel floor below, bringing many regular Enforcement bots along with it.

"Cago on standby for target three," Flynn heard. He looked up at the ceiling.

"Initiate target three."

Then, as according to plan, Cago stopped using his powers and suddenly appeared above the juggernaut, stuck upside down on what was left of the intersection's ceiling. Silently, he dropped an explosive onto the back of the juggernaut's short neck.

As it engaged it made a small beeping noise before exploding, causing the troops surrounding the juggernaut to look up. Because it had landed slightly off target, it hadn't done much damage, but had only caused a distraction. Which is all they needed.

Cago gave them enough time to see he was there, then used his powers to dissolve into the shadows, disappearing from sight. The Enforcement soldiers opened fire, but were shooting at nothing but cement, so they stopped and listened, guns sweeping the room as they tried their best to sense their prey.

A few moments later, Cago flashed into view on the floor of an adjacent intersection. The soldiers spotted him but instead of firing they ran in pursuit after the now invisible Cago.

Flynn looked up at the gigantic, nearly uninjured robot and held his breath. In order for this to work, the juggernaut had to follow the rest of the soldiers.

It paused before slowly turning and stomping after the rest of the robots.

Flynn exhaled. "And again," he said to himself. "Proof that Bi's tactical skills never fail."

Tarff stood atop a skyscraper, looking down at the battle raging below. There were only robots in the streets on both sides for miles. Sending a human in would be suicide.

Tarff watched as the explosions went off and the road collapsed beneath the two juggernauts. "Both targets are under." He said.

"Affirmative. Move to position three."

Tarff looked down at the figure of Blackeye, who was in a prone position on the roof, her sniper rifle pointed at some unknown point down below.

"You're going to be okay by yourself, right?" Tarff asked.

Blackeye didn't move or give any other recognition, but Tarff knew she had heard him. Blackeye heard everything.

Tarff walked over to the side of the skyscraper and looked down at the alleyway hundreds of feet below, where a small group of Enforcement soldiers were waiting for commands. Now that there were less robots in the streets, he could finally move in to help the others in the fight. "Here goes nothing," he mumbled. Taking a deep breath, he jumped off.

He fell for a few mere seconds, definitely not enjoying the ground speeding up towards him.

As he hit the ground, his abilities kicked in and he felt his muscles bulge from the quick rush of energy. The seemingly unsurprised robot soldiers turned and began firing at Tarff's rapidly growing figure. The shots did nothing.

Tarff charged into the group in front of him, brutally punching or throwing any bot that stood in his way until they were all turned into scrap heaps on the ground.

Looking to his left, he saw another group of soldiers run into the alley. He then turned and ran to the far end of the alleyway, where it ended with a wall. Reaching down, he wrenched a manhole cover out of the ground, bolts and all, and threw it at the nearest soldier, ripping it in half along with any that were behind it. *So that's how Flynn does it,* he thought.

Moving quickly, Tarff shrunk his body down slightly and jumped down the drain right as more soldiers filled the alley.

He swiftly moved into the shadows of the pipe and watched as the heads of many robots filled the hole where the only light was flowing through. Using the darkness to his advantage, he bolted down the sewage pipe, away from his enemies. Looking behind him, he saw Enforcement bots dropping down into the tunnel and firing after him, drawing even more enemies underground. His plan had worked.

No, he thought. *Not my plan. Bi's.*

Flynn dove behind a pile of boxes and began reloading. After the juggernaut had fallen into their trap, Cago had led it down into the largest of all the intersections, where they had previously set up defensive turrets and barricades. They were now desperately trying to hurt the massive robot, but it was taking a while and hadn't been very effective.

Having reloaded his gun, he peeked back out from behind the crate and began firing. The juggernaut was facing away from him, but there were also many supporting Enforcement troops that fanned around it in every direction, making it difficult to get a shot at the beast.

Flynn had realized that many of Clan Pris' long-range specialists were having a hard time in such close-quarters combat, meaning he and Cago were this group's best hope. And that by itself was a scary thought.

Flynn ran over to another barricade, leveling every robot in his way before sliding behind cover.

"Nice," a modified, mechanical-sounding voice said.

Flynn turned and saw a member of Clan Pris next to him, his sniper rifle pointed through a hole in the boxes. "Thanks."

"They call me Split," he said. "Andromeda sent me and Nebula here to watch over you and Cago."

Nebula, who had previously been cloaked, flashed into view for a brief moment before quickly disappearing. When he listened closely, he could distinguish the sound of her gun firing from a few feet away.

Flynn spun and leveled his gun atop one of the crates, firing into the enemy lines. He shot until he ran out of bullets, ducking back behind the crate to reload.

"You're a pretty good shot for a junior," Split said. His tone sounded more like he was relaxing on a beach, not like he was shooting something that might kill him at any moment.

"Thanks," Flynn said.

"So you're from Sacramento?" he asked. Flynn was confused at why he was talking to him in the middle of the battle. Maybe it was his way of coping with the action.

"Yep," Flynn said. "Lived there my whole life." He realized that he began to calm down a bit himself. Maybe he should do this more often. "Where are you from?"

"Before the war?" he asked. "Florida. I would go surf with all of my friends there. Nebula and I grew up on the same street too. I was sort of hoping that living in Florida would help me get a chance of being in Clan Troy but..." He shrugged. "No such luck."

"Why would you want to be in Clan Troy?" Flynn asked as he reloaded again. He was noticing that being calm had helped his accuracy slightly.

He shrugged. "I have always dreamed of fighting to save something. And dying if necessary."

Nebula flashed back into view. "Are you just going to keep talking to him about how heroic you allegedly are or are we going to come up with a plan? This doesn't seem to be working."

Flynn looked around the area. She was right. They didn't seem to be making much progress. "Bi said we need to get it to the east corner of the intersection," Flynn responded. The juggernaut was currently in the middle, closer to the west side of the intersection.

"How are you going to do that?" Split asked.

"We need to distract it." Flynn thought for a moment, and an idea came to him. "Can you two clear a path to the juggernaut for me?"

Split fired off a couple of rounds and tossed a grenade forward. "Already have."

Flynn quickly spun around the side of the barricade and ran towards the juggernaut, dodging bullets from enemies and friends as he made his way towards the center of the area. Running fast, he leapt through the air and grabbed onto the lower part of the giant robot's back.

Now hanging nearly ten feet above the ground, Flynn placed his feet on the metal plates on the robot's back and began climbing. As he neared the top, one of his feet slipped and he lost his grip. As he fell, he quickly grabbed onto a metal fiber tube that was hanging on the outside of the juggernaut. Taking a deep breath, he began climbing again.

Once he made it to the top, he pulled an explosive charge out from his belt and placed it on the back of the juggernaut's head. Then, after climbing down halfway, he jumped off the back of the robot and landed softly, igniting the explosives as he hit the ground.

The explosion made the juggernaut stumble forward and it turned to face its attacker. Perfect.

Flynn took multiple steps backward, brandishing his staff as if to mock the large robot. He continued to keep his eyes on the other Enforcement troops near him, who were hesitantly closing in, many being dropped to the ground by his comrades. The juggernaut stepped forward and raised his arm, firing at Flynn with its wrist-mounted gun. Spinning his staff, Flynn easily deflected the bullets to the side. "Come on! Is that the best you can do?"

Making a mechanical grunting noise, the juggernaut charged.

And so did Tarff.

He came smashing through a wall and into the intersection, ramming into the side of the juggernaut. Having now changed to be about the same size as the mechanical beast, he smashed it into the side of the intersection.

A cheer rose up from the human soldiers as the juggernaut again got thrown into the wall before getting pummeled in the face by Tarff's four powerful fists.

As it struggled to regain balance, Tarff began shoving it farther towards the corner that Bi had directed them to get it to. The corner where the explosives would collapse the ceiling in on the robot, hopefully destroying it.

Flynn and the rest of the twenty or so people from Clan Pris began overpowering the Enforcement bots as their numbers started to diminish. He ran back to the place where Nebula and Split were waiting for him. "That thing is tough," Flynn said as he reached them and dove for cover, pulling out a gun so he could help in the fight.

"Your explosion seemed effective," Split said. "We should try some more. Nebula and I have more powerful ones than you. With all that we have, we might be able to kill it."

"Bi has given us specific orders," Flynn said. "We need to follow her plan."

"Why?" Split asked. "There can be other alternatives."

"Because we need to trust Bi," Nebula said. "We can't win this war if we are fighting against each other."

"Well-" Split stopped, glancing at Nebula before adjusting his posture. "Of course. That is an excellent idea. Couldn't have said it better myself. So what's the plan, Flynn?"

Flynn looked confusedly between the two soldiers. Both had the Andromeda symbol on their shoulder plate. If they were in a squad together then they were obviously friends but for a second Flynn wondered if maybe... Nevermind. It didn't matter. "The ceiling is going to be our weapon here. When the bot gets in the corner we give the signal and it gets crushed."

All three of them looked to where the bot was wrestling with Tarff, steadily moving back towards the corner.

"We've got it!" Split said. At that moment, the juggernaut looked at the corner he was being backed into and then at the ceiling. If understanding could come to the robot's mechanical eyes, it just did.

"Spoke too soon," Split said as the robot shoved his way through Tarff and towards the center of the room.

Without hesitating, Nebula rushed forward, sprinting straight towards the juggernaut.

"No!" Split half reached out to her before realizing she was far past him and she probably wouldn't listen anyways.

Like a professional acrobat, Nebula leapt through the air and landed, hanging on the juggernaut's back. Without missing a beat, she scaled its back in seconds.

"Wish I could have done that," Flynn mumbled to himself.

Nebula began trying to distract it long enough for Tarff to recover, but it had figured out the plan. And they didn't have a back up.

Flynn saw a group of snipers appear down one of the tunnels. Among them was Cago and Andromeda, along with a tall, elegant woman in solid white armor, accented with purple highlights.

The juggernaut turned to face the group of newcomers and raised his gun.

Acting swiftly, Split sprinted towards them, standing defensively in front of the tunnel and putting himself between the newcomers and the huge robot. Flynn watched a flicker of approval in the white one's posture before she turned back to the danger in front of them.

Tarff began to stand up, but the juggernaut turned its gun towards him and fired. It did no damage to Tarff, but his suit was getting shredded and he was being pushed into the ground. His power was diminishing, and they were running out of time.

The juggernaut kept its gun focused on Tarff but began walking towards Split, raising a spiked fist.

Split valiantly pulled a grenade and a small piece of paper out from his belt and raised them into the air, mocking the robot toward him and away from the tunnel where Cago, Andromeda, and who Flynn guessed was Captain Pris were. Didn't Split know his grenade wouldn't do anything to the juggernaut? He was going to die for nothing. And he seemingly didn't care.

At that moment Flynn realized no one could get there in time. Split was doomed.

The juggernaut raised his massive fist in the air, and with one swift motion, brought it down onto Split's small form.

It never made it.

The back of the juggernaut's head exploded, starting a chain reaction of explosions out of its back. Pieces of metal flew from its spine, along with the figure of a small person, who landed roughly, her body sprawled on the ground.

As the juggernaut collapsed in multiple pieces across the room, Split dropped his grenade, luckily still not activated, and sprinted over to the person on the ground. Flynn saw the small piece of paper flutter out of his hand as he ran.

Walking slowly over to it, he picked the piece of paper up. It was a picture of Nebula while still in her junior squad years before now. She had her helmet in her left hand and her right arm around Split, both of them smiling happily at the camera.

Flynn looked up at Split, who was partially out of view by the people currently gathered around him.

Flynn approached him, walking through the small crowd and kneeling by his side. Nebula was sitting against one of the cement walls, her face holding a sad smile as she looked up at Split.

"This is the way to go," she said.

"Don't say that," Split cut in.

"Just because I'm about to die doesn't mean I'm going to start listening to you." She smiled more. "This is how I always wanted to die. Valiantly for a noble cause. And now here I am. Surrounded by friends. With you." She reached out and gently grabbed his hand. "At least-" She struggled to say her final words. "I got a hero's send-off."

She let out her last breath.

"She was one of our best."

Flynn turned to the woman in white armor behind him.

"Captain Pris," one of the soldiers said. Flynn could tell everyone held her in high respect."Why have you left the skyscrapers?"

"The war down here is far more important than up there," Pris said. "Besides, the upper streets are desolate."

"Why?" Split asked.

"A battleship crashed into the shore this morning. Part of the engine was broken when Sergeant Bi disabled the cannons. When they used the engine again it exploded, destroying a lot of the boat and most of its inhabitants. When this news got to the soldiers, they raced to protect their larger brethren down here in the tunnels. We destroyed their reinforcements. Thanks to you guys, and especially Nebula, half of their current forces are gone."

"Well," Split stood up and put his helmet on. "Let's go take out the other half."

Pris looked back at him. "Split-"

"I have had enough here." He looked down at Nebula's hand, which held an identical copy of the folded picture that Flynn had picked up. The same hand that had been holding his, full of life, just seconds ago. "She wouldn't have wanted us to wait around and let more people die." For a few seconds no one said anything. Split slung his sniper rifle over his shoulder, took one more look at Nebula, and began walking away.

Everyone else looked over at Split and then down at Nebula's dead body. Then, slowly, they began following him down the tunnel.

The battle seemed to be over before it started. It was merely minutes after Captain Pris and the others arrived that the robots were defeated and the second juggernaut was crushed by the collapsed ceiling. Flynn later found out from Tarff that Blackeye and another sniper from Clan Pris had been waiting on two nearby rooftops, ready to shoot the explosives manually on command instead of using a trigger, which minimized the odds of a malfunction. Apparently she had landed the shot.

The streets above were now empty, a stark contrast to the previous battlefield that used to fill them.

By the time sunrise hit, Flynn and the others were packing their things away and were getting ready to leave.

"Hey Flynn, you got everything packed up?" Cago asked, slinging his backpack over his shoulder.

"Almost." Flynn pulled something from his belt to place in his backpack. As he did, the picture from earlier fluttered to the ground. He had picked it up on the way out of the sewers, and had forgotten to return it to Split.

"On second thought, tell Bi I'm going to be a minute," Flynn told Cago.

"Where are you going?" he asked.

"To investigate something." Flynn walked down the hallway of the office building they were currently inside, turned to the right, and began walking up the stairs. After the third set, he came to a door leading onto the roof. He pulled at the handle. Locked.

Reaching out with his mind, Flynn began moving pieces inside the lock mechanism. After a few seconds, he heard a small click.

Silently, Flynn opened the door. The rooftop was simple, gray concrete. It overlooked the Hudson River and was so tall you could see in all directions for miles. Seated on the edge was Split. His helmet was off, but Flynn thought it could pass for just this once.

"Nice job unlocking the door," he said before Flynn even moved. "I am a blackeye, meaning I can sense things even when I can't see them. Nebula had a similar ability, as do lots of people in our clan. Come, sit down." He gestured beside him.

Flynn walked forward and sat beside the soldier. "We have a blackeye in our group. She is also a healer."

"I noticed," he said. "Not so good at coming up with nicknames I suppose?"

Flynn chuckled. "Ryan comes up with most of them. Besides, we know nothing else about her. She never talks to anyone."

"I see." He paused for a moment, looking out into the distance, "Losing someone close to you is hard, Flynn. You and I both know that from experience."

Flynn looked over at him, surprised. He smiled. "I have my ways of finding out things. Me and Bi have spoken before."

Flynn handed him the picture he had picked up on the battlefield. "Thought you might want this."

Split unfolded it and looked at it for a few moments. He still looked the same as he had in the picture, his soft blonde hair sticking up all over the place. It contrasted hers, which was done neatly, the color a bright purple, just like Clan Pris. "The trials are far from over yet, Flynn," he said. "Take this." He handed Flynn the picture. "So you can remember what has been lost, but most importantly so you can remember how much power we have to gain our freedom."

As Flynn stood up to leave, he heard Split call out to him. "And Flynn, try to stay alive. We still have a war to win."

His own life. Flynn wished that was what he cared about most.

INTERLUDE

11- Purifiers

Northern Minnesota
United States
6:30 p.m.
James

James could feel every single bump on the frozen ground as the Lander's wheels traveled over them. It was extremely cold in the small sitting area in the back of the Lander and, despite it still being June, frost was clinging to the fabric walls. James had actually studied Landers for a few months back when he was thirty, before he became a footsoldier and was working as one of Xion's engineers. He had even built a few of the vehicles himself so he knew exactly where every piece went. Their actual name was "Armored Troop Carriers," which was a pretty good description considering they carried artillery and soldiers across land.

"Hey Bolter." James perked up at the sound of his name and turned to look at Broadside, a fellow soldier in James' squad. "How many do you think I'll get this time?"

James thought for a moment. "Do you mean robots or girls once you get back to the base?"

The other soldiers in the Lander chuckled, but Broadside was used to these jokes. "Both."

"I'd say..." James paused. "About thirty."

Broadside smiled. "I could live with that."

"I'll wager twenty," Decker interjected. Decker was their heavyweight and by far the largest soldier in their squad. "No more than that."

"For how much?" Broadside asked.

"Drinks for the rest of us."

James smiled. This is what war was about. Betting on how good you would do in a fight and fighting that much harder so you wouldn't have to buy drinks for the rest of the squad, who could drink for hours.

"You have yourself a deal," Broadside said, extending his hand. "I get less than twenty and we all get drinks on me."

Decker shook his hand. "I can taste them already."

They all cheered even though they all knew Broadside could do it. He was the kind of guy who you always wanted on your team and as a friend. To James he was almost like an older brother.

The small metal panel between the cab and the back area of the Lander slid open and Sarge's face came into view. "We're approaching our target, men. Stand ready."

James and the twelve other soldiers all prepped their suits and checked their equipment. The enemy outpost they were going to was supposedly a facility that was designing a structure for a new tank. Considering the members of Clan Xion were engineering specialists, it made sense that they were the ones sent on this mission to steal the Enforcement's plans. The plans were most likely somewhere in a digital file bank, which meant James would be the one to extract it. That put all the weight on his shoulders, and he was fine with that.

James had always loved fighting. As a teen he would get in fights all the time and, unlike most of the people he fought, he enjoyed it. Some of the other soldiers did it for their lives, Broadside did it for the ladies, but James did it for fun. He loved the thrill of the fight. The adrenaline.

"Target is incoming," Their driver, Ingus, said. "Only 2.5 kilometers until we engage."

"Belca, man the gun," Sarge said from the front seat.

One of the soldiers stood up and strode to the middle of the cramped space, where a metal block protruded from the floor. He stepped up onto it, ducking his head into a metal dome that stuck out of the roof. He then grabbed two handles that stuck out of the ceiling. The controls for a turret.

"One kilometer and closing." Ingus began flipping switches and the soldiers began to shift in their seats. For a moment there was silence. Then the guns began firing.

Without their suits, the soldiers would have been deafened by now. Belca was firing like mad from the turret mounted atop the Lander, his precision shooting taking out the dozens of guards that were shooting back at him. Ingus slammed on the brakes and drifted sideways, setting up the Lander in a defensive position as a barricade.

"File out," Sarge barked. "And remember your assignments!"

The group filed out through the back of the vehicle and onto the opposite side of the Lander, ducking behind it as cover.

"Squad Delta," Ingus said over their in-suit speakers. "Initiate attack."

With their guns ready, the soldiers ran out from behind the vehicle, shooting at whatever guards remained before running towards the base.

It was a small, two-story outpost in the shape of a pentagon. Based on the lack of exterior guards and various loading bays, James could tell without a doubt that this was a factory.

The squad split off into five groups of two or three members, each one going to a different entrance.

James, who was with Broadside and Sarge, took the main door. When they arrived, James pulled out his gadgets and began working to get the door open. The panel was difficult to hack but it was Enforcement technology, and

James had seen similar panels many times before. Compared to Clan Xion's equipment, this was nothing.

After a few seconds, the metal panels slid aside with a hiss, revealing five guards standing with their guns raised. Broadside leveled his gatling gun and shredded bullets through the robots, their own guns being nearly ineffective to his suit.

"Five," Broadside said as they ran through the doorway. Sarge led them down the hall, toward one of the many information storage rooms. As they neared it, two more patrol guards came into view but were down before they could even fire.

"Seven."

Two more guards were in front of the room's door, and James managed to stab one with his electric knife before Broadside took out the other one.

"Eight."

James ran into the room, speeding through the aisles of data storage shelves. It was dark, the small LEDs on the storage computer towers being the only light sources in the room.

Near the back of the room he found the main tower and plugged his corrolis splinching tool into it. He watched as the piece of technology searched for the file, downloading anything that might be important.

"Nothing," he said.

"Next room!" Sarge led them down more tunnel-like hallways before arriving at a staircase. They ran up the stairs and shoved open the door at the top, only to find a barricade in front of them. Sarge slammed the door closed again as gunfire rained towards them.

"Blast it!" Sarge cursed. "They are guarding this floor heavily. It has to be up here. Prepare grenades!"

James pulled a grenade from his belt and held his knife in his other hand.

"Three," Sarge put a hand on the door. "Two, one!"

He pushed the door open and the torrent broke loose. James threw his grenade which destroyed a few bots but they were quickly replaced by new ones.

"Eat this!" Broadside blasted away with his gun, dropping soldier after soldier, but it wasn't enough.

"We need to get through!" Sarge yelled. "Follow me." He tossed a grenade forward and charged in as it blasted a hole through the enemies' barricade. Broadside and James ran with him.

Once past the barricade, Sarge slammed through a door on the left. Another file room.

"Block the door!" Sarge barked. He began to move anything he could find towards it.

"Bolter, find the file!" Broadside yelled. "We've got this."

James sprinted as fast as he could to the back of the room, and took out his tools to work.

"Come on, come on," he said as the corrolis splinching tool began searching. He could hear robots trying to barge through the door.

Suddenly another door behind James opened. He quickly pulled out his knife before seeing the other ten members of his squad stumble through, more gunfire coming from behind them. Decker quickly grabbed an entire shelf of storage towers and shoved it in front of the door.

James watched as a green light blinked on his wrist. "I've got the file!" he announced, and a cheer went up from the soldiers. Many of the newcomers were injured, and one couldn't even walk.

"Signals are down," Sarge said as the group gathered in the middle of the large room, a continuous banging still coming from the two doors. "We can't contact anyone and we're surrounded. Any ideas?"

One of the soldiers was about to say something when Sarge cut in. "No, we aren't using the ventilation system, Marcus. Don't you remember how that went last time?"

A shiver ran through the group. Of course they remembered what happened last time. Most probably wished they could forget.

There was a loud noise and James spun to see that a few robots had begun to break their way through the wall, their metal hands reaching through like zombies'.

"We're running out of options here," Decker said.

All eyes were on Sarge, who stood still, unsure of what to do as the robots continued to try and enter the room.

There was a loud bang on the door and the whole room shook. It shook again. The squad of soldiers began to back up. Another bang.

Then silence.

James stepped forward and looked through the tiny window in the door. What he saw surprised him. The Enforcement troopers were backing down the hall, guns firing at an unseen enemy.

James looked to where their guns were pointed and was confused until he saw it. Coming through the barricade, looking like a group of dragon-steel armored angels, was the Purifier Squad.

The Purifier Squad was the best squad in Clan Xion, similar to the elite guards of Captains Troy or Dax, except these guys worked alone. Three disciplined and high-skilled troopers with flame throwers with elegant armor and the power to take on hundreds of robots at once.

The fourth, however, was an explosive-crazy lunatic that they dragged out of an insane asylum. Or so the rumors went. James had no idea how many of them were true, but he knew that the stories of them were legendary.

James jumped back from the door, squinting his eyes as the hallway erupted in flames, the bulletproof window melting from the heat. Another cheer went up from the earlier defeated soldiers as they began to unblockade the door.

The Purifier Squad finished off all of the enemies in the hallway quickly and came inside with the rest of the soldiers.

"Admiral Scorch," Sarge said confidently. "The timing of your arrival is excellent."

"Thank you Sergeant," Scorch replied. The three soldiers towered above all the others, even Decker. "Do your forces wish to continue with the fight?"

Another cheer rose up and James chuckled. This is why he loved his squad. Everything was a game to them.

"Very well," Scorch turned to his soldiers. "Inferno, you take these troops to the east section of the compound. Blaze, you will come with me to the North. Croucher, you know what your orders are."

A small, hunchbacked soldier hobbled from behind the three towering Purifiers, looking up at his sergeant as he cackled wildly, his voice raspy and strained. "Any specifics?"

"We have no quarter," Scorch said. "We leave no survivors."

Croucher let out another deranged laugh. "That is what I like to hear."

"Come on men," Sarge said. "Today we will taste victory!" A final cheer rose up from all of the soldiers.

"Hey Broadside," Decker said as they began to follow Inferno out of the room. "How many did you get?"

"Thirty-four," he answered as he reloaded his massive gun with a new magazine. "But don't worry. After what happened today, I'll get you your drinks anyways."

PART II

TRUST ISSUES

12- Party

The Warehouse, Sacramento
California, USA
5:30 pm
Flynn

The air was cool on the deck overlooking the city. Flynn was relaxing on a chair, water glass in hand, trying to figure out what to do. The summer had started three weeks ago, and since then, no new reports from the war had come out. Flynn almost felt bored.

He heard the glass door behind him slide open. Bi walked towards one of the chairs on the deck and sat down. "Zane is almost done with his new upgrade to Proxy, and Tarff is back from football practice now."

"Huh," Flynn said as he took another drink of his water.

"You seem mellow," she commented.

"Wow," Flynn said sarcastically. "She does it again. The great Sergeant Bi, reader of minds." He sipped his drink again.

Bi chuckled. "Actually, I thought I might have something that might cheer you up."

"A mission?" Flynn said.

"Kind of."

"Is it dangerous?" he asked.

"Also kind of," Bi replied.

"What is it?"

"I want you to go to a party."

Flynn stared at her. "A party? Bi, we are in the middle of a war. Not only would that be unproductive, it is also dangerous. I could be found."

"I am simply asking you, Flynn," she said, "I am not forcing you to go."

"Is this one of your tests?" Flynn wondered.

"No."

"Then why do you want me to go so badly?"

"I just find these situations amusing."

"What situations?"

"Emily will be there."

Flynn paused "You wanted to get me to go against the idea of going to a party so you could study my reaction when you mention a girl's name. Clever, but predictable." He paused. "It also isn't going to change my mind one bit." He set his drink down and stood up to leave.

"Then where are you going?" Bi asked.

Flynn turned back around and smiled. "To the party, of course."

"I really don't like you right now Flynn," Cago said. He was seated next to Flynn in the back seat of the Lamborghini. His normally messy hair was combed, and, instead of his typical black on black, he was wearing a plaid red and blue button-up with jeans. Flynn had opted for a more casual khakis with a T-shirt.

"You've never been to a party before," Flynn said. "You need to get to know people."

"Oh, I've been to a few parties," Cago replied. "But all I do is stand off to the side for a couple of hours after giving up on trying to be social."

"Come on," Flynn said. "It can't be that bad. I expect you to talk to at least ten people." He paused. Then he added, "And five of them have to be girls."

Cago stiffened. "Out of the question."

Flynn laughed. "Just be casual. It'll be alright."

"Fine," Cago gave in. "But I expect you to talk to twenty."

"Done," Flynn said. "Although don't expect me to stick around them for long."

"Why not?"

"I have a very specific girl I want to talk to."

The car slowed as they arrived. The party, although hosted by Trevor, was at Dom's house, which was massive. Dom's parents let people use their house as long as they paid a pretty good price and didn't damage anything. Tons of people filled the house and the front yard.

Blackeye, who was driving, pressed a button that unlocked and opened the two back doors. They were butterfly doors, so they went up into the air instead of out. Flynn and Cago exited the vehicle as Blackeye closed the doors and drove away.

"Well," Cago drew in a deep breath. "Here goes nothing."

The house looked even bigger from the inside. People were everywhere. Most of them Flynn recognized from his high school, but some were unfamiliar. The main room was massive and two stories tall, along with it being connected to many other rooms. It was extremely loud because of all of the people talking along with the blaring music in the background.

Flynn saw a couple of girls he recognized. "Mia! Abby!" They turned towards him and he beckoned them over. He smiled as they approached. "Girls, this is Cago. You probably don't know him, but he goes to our school."

Both of them looked over at him and Flynn could tell he wanted to shrink into the crowd.

"Oh," Abby said. "I know you! I sat next to you in biology!"

"Really?" Cago said.

"Yeah," she said. "Don't you remember? We had Miss Gill and-"

"No," Cago said. "I r-remember you, I just didn't think you would know who I was."

"Of course I know you," Abby said. "You're so cool!"

Cago froze. "Um... Thanks."

"Oh, there's Trevor," Abby paused and adjusted her hair before grabbing Mia's arm. "Nice seeing you again Cago!"

The two boys watched them leave.

"That wasn't too bad," Flynn said, nudging Cago in the arm. "She was kind of interested in you."

"I'm so surprised she remembered me," Cago said.

"Not Abby," Flynn chuckled. "Did you not notice Mia? Mia is normally more energetic than Abby is! She's only shy when she's around Trevor."

"Really?" Cago asked.

"And she couldn't take her eyes off you."

"Really?" he said again.

"See for yourself."

Although Flynn was facing in the opposite direction of where the girls had gone, Cago looked back over his shoulder to find that he was right. From across the room, through the crowds of people, the girls were talking with Trevor and his friends, but Mia kept glancing over her shoulder back at Cago. When she noticed that he was looking she stopped and pretended to not see him and go back into the conversation.

"Maybe she just saw something on my clothes." Cago adjusted his collar and searched his shirt and pants for any stains or other things that might be out of place.

"Yeah, right," Flynn said.

"Is she still looking?"

"Yep."

"You can't even see them."

"Check if you want to."

Cago turned back toward them. This time she blushed before looking down at the ground.

"How did you know?" he asked.

Flynn smiled. "People are predictable. Now come on. You need to give Mia some time to wonder if you even know she exists before you go back and talk to her. Besides, you still have five girls to meet."

"Five?" Cago asked. "I just met two."

"Those technically counted on my score," Flynn corrected. "We can't both get credit for the same girls."

Cago huffed and folded his arms as he looked around the room. "I'm going to go talk to Olivia. She's nice and is surrounded by at least twenty people."

"Not if I get there first."

Flynn and Cago looked at each other for a second, then started pushing their way through the crowd of people, racing to get to where Olivia stood.

Suddenly, Flynn saw a glint out of the corner of his eye and paused, turning toward it. When he saw what it was, he froze.

Standing twenty feet away from him, her dark brown hair falling past her shoulders, wearing light blue jeans and a purple shirt, was Emily.

"On second thought," Flynn said to Cago, "you can take them all."

As Flynn began making his way to where Emily was, she looked up and saw him. She waved to him and smiled.

Flynn almost collapsed on the floor. Even though he was so confident while convincing Cago to talk to girls, when it came to Emily, he was clueless. Maybe that is why he liked her so much.

"I was beginning to wonder if you were going to come," she said as he arrived.

"What could I possibly be doing that could make me want to miss this?" Flynn asked.

"I thought your parents might not let you come," she replied.

"Luckily, no." Flynn had told all of his friends that his parents were very strict, which often helped if he needed an excuse to be gone.

"Come on," Emily said. "I have something I want to show you."

She walked out of the main room and up some stairs.

"Where are we going?" he asked.

"Patience," she smiled. "You'll find out soon enough."

After what seemed like an eternity of weaving through hallways and staircases throughout the massive house, they made it to a glass door. Emily opened it and led Flynn out onto a deck.

Because the house was so far from the city, no pollution filled the air and stars filled the sky.

He looked around for a moment before turning back to Emily who was gazing up at the sky. "It's beautiful isn't it?" she said.

"Yeah, sure is."

She looked back at Flynn. "I was talking about the stars."

"Oh." He looked back up. "I guess they are a little bit."

She smiled and slapped him in the arm.

"I'm guessing I deserved that," Flynn said. This is where he really wanted to be. The battlefield was exhilarating, but after a while, you got used to it. But being with Emily however, Flynn didn't think he would ever get used to that.

They sat down on one of the two outdoor couches that were placed on the deck. He felt his insides bursting as he realized how close he was to her right now. He felt like he was going to explode.

Flynn heard a whistle from the yard below and a shower of sparks burst out in front of him. Fireworks. It took Flynn a second to realize that it was Independence Day. While you were in a civil war, it was easy to forget about those types of things.

Flynn glanced over at Emily. She had no clue what was going on out there. He could have died multiple times at war, and she had no idea. Flynn probably would never be able to tell her. First of all, she didn't know he was Ironborn, and secondly, even if she did know, she would worry too much. He hated it when Emily was worried. He hated seeing someone so perfectly amazing be upset about something. Especially when it was something he could never fix. At least he could still try to make her happy.

Emily looked over and noticed he was staring at her. She started laughing.

"What?" Flynn wondered.

"Nothing." She shook her head. "You are a very special person Flynn."

"In what way?" Flynn asked.

"A way," she said.

"Wow," Flynn chuckled. "That helps a lot." He paused for a few moments. "How did you know about this place anyway?" He motioned to the deck around him.

"One of Trevor's friends showed it to me," she replied.

"Trevor's friend as in a boy or a girl?" Flynn asked.

She looked over at him curiously. "Does it matter?"

Flynn froze. "No no, not at all."

She laughed again. “A girl, Flynn. In fact, I think she is going to come up here soon.”

At that moment, the door behind them opened and Mia came through with Cago behind her.

Emily was surprised. “I thought you were planning on coming with Trevor.”

“I was but I got...” she glanced over at Cago, “Sidetracked.”

“I see,” Emily smiled. “You can sit with us if you like.”

“Thanks.” Mia and Cago sat down on the deck next to them. All of them were watching the fireworks except for Flynn. Sitting there, watching Emily smile, was all he wanted to do.

It was nearly midnight when Mia's mom pulled up to take the two girls home. After the fireworks were over, the foursome had gone for a walk down the neighborhood streets for about two hours.

They all hugged each other and said goodbye as Mia got into the car and Emily followed after her.

“Hey Flynn,” Emily said, pausing outside the car. “I heard that they are doing this again in two weeks. Same time, same place. Can you come?”

“I’d love to,” he replied.

“You can come if you want to Cago.” Mia said from inside the car.

“O-ok,” Cago stammered.

Emily walked to the car, waving to Flynn one last time before getting inside and being driven away.

As the car pulled out from in front of Cago and Flynn, they saw a person standing on the sidewalk across the road, clad in black and red armor, a captain's symbol embossed into the left side of the soldier's breastplate.

“Captain Vilo,” Flynn said, surprised. “To what do we owe this unexpected visit?”

“I came here with a message.” Vilo’s voice was as confident as ever. She walked toward them. “Considering your situation,” she gestured in the direction of where the vehicle had left, “I opted to wait until they were gone. I would hate to steal a perfect night away from you, Flynn. She truly is beautiful.”

Flynn bowed his head slightly. “Thank you Captain. You said you had a message?”

“Yes,” she continued. “An assignment, actually.”

“Really?” Flynn perked up.

“Yes,” she said. “Allow me to ask you a question. How much do you know about project 1711?”

"You're kidding." Flynn felt excitement rise inside of him. Finally.

"No Flynn, I'm not kidding." Her voice was neutral. "You are to study project 1711 under the direction of Sergeant Bi."

"Oh I think he is already studying her enough, Captain." Cago chuckled.

Vilo moved her gaze over to him.

"Sorry Captain," he coughed and looked down at the ground.

Vilo looked back to Flynn.

"Thank you," he said. "It will be an honor to take this assignment. When do I start?"

"Well," she started, "if my information is not false, you will be seeing her again in two weeks. You shall start then."

"Thank you again, Captain," Flynn said. "I'll be looking forward to it."

13- Training

The Warehouse, Sacramento
California, USA
12:30 pm
Flynn

"His maneuvering is quick but he needs more skill with weapons," Bi said. "Considering our weapons trainer is unable to teach, Zane will fill in her spot."

Zane, Flynn, Tarff and Bi were standing behind the one-way pane of glass, watching as Cago struggled to get past the simulation. Ryan and Blackeye were also currently training in a two-person simulation that could be viewed on the other side of the room, but no one was paying attention to them.

"He never uses anything except his knife," Zane said. "Why is he so arrogant?"

"He thinks this knife is special," Bi answered. "It has saved his life many times, along with it being the only item he still holds that was his father's."

Zane nodded in understanding. "Should I train him in other things?"

"Yes," Bi said. "There will probably be a time when he will need it." She pressed a button. "Cago, we are going to try something." She let go of the button.

"What are you doing?" Flynn wondered.

"A test." She flipped some switches and restarted the system. In front of the glass, Zane saw a half dozen figures appear. The projections were shadowy and each held a knife in both hands.

Cago smiled and drew his dull, gray knife from around his neck as they approached. Ryan noted that he held his knife backhand, making it harder to see.

"He's mocking them," Flynn said.

Bi pressed another button and one of the projections jumped towards him and the others charged.

Cago slashed his blade around wildly, dropping one projection after another. They were gone in seconds, their shadowy bodies fading out of existence as their assassin clipped his knife back into the thin chain around his neck. Cago came out without a scratch.

"Amazing," Zane said.

"Well," Flynn commented, "he has skill with one weapon."

"I want to speak with Flynn," Bi said to Zane. "Continue with his training. I want you to find his limit."

"Yes sergeant."

Flynn followed Bi out of the viewing room and out into the hallway that accessed the bedrooms.

"You're thinking about her again," Bi said as they walked down the stairs.

"What makes you say that?" Flynn asked.

"I have my ways of figuring things out," she said. "Besides, I have seen that look before."

"Should I try to not think about her?"

"Well," Bi started, "you should think about other things sometimes, of course, but I wonder what would happen if she discovered your secret. If she means that much to you, it could be devastating."

"I believe she is a supporter of the Ironborn," Flynn said.

Bi eyed him. "Are you sure?"

"Pretty sure," Flynn said reluctantly.

"So she is just a normal person then?"

"No, because she could be-" Flynn paused. "You already know all this."

"Possibly," she said. "Even if I did, it is good for you to say it outloud. It makes it easier for you to process things."

Flynn nodded.

"We got a report from Clan Xion."

"About what?"

"They found a new technology that the Industry is trying to develop," she said. "They call it a Stingray. It is a tank-like vehicle."

"Interesting." Flynn paused. "You tell me this, why?"

"This tank is designed for front-line soldiers. That is your specialty."

"So you want me to learn how to defeat one?"

"Yes." She led him to a computer. "This will be your task for today. First study it until a training room is open. Then get to the physical training."

"I'm on it sergant."

She began to walk away before turning around. "Flynn."

"Yes?"

"I'll have some news for you when you are done."

It took Flynn hours to get it right, but he finally defeated a Stingray. After running through the data and schematics with Zane, they were able to make a replication of it in the virtual training room. He discovered that the weaponry on the vehicle was a single top-mounted ray gun, with the ability to nearly vaporize most materials. Hopefully Tarff would be around if Flynn had to face one in real life.

Flynn walked down to the kitchen to find three empty boxes of pizza on the counter, along with a plate with four slices that were left for him, even though he couldn't eat more than two. Bi was seated at the table, scrolling through something on her laptop, and she looked up as he walked in.

"You finished your training," she noted.

"That thing wasn't easy to take down." Flynn said, sitting down at the table. "Either Zane over-programmed the simulation or some of our soldiers are going to have a pretty hard time."

"Any weak points?" Bi inquired.

Flynn shrugged. "Same as most of the other tanks. Anything that moves."

Bi nodded. "Makes sense."

Flynn took a bite of pizza. "You said you had news for me?"

"That's right." Bi looked up at him. "Flynn, I've been thinking about this for a while and I have decided that I want to make you the lieutenant of our squad."

Flynn choked on his pizza. "Lieutenant?"

Bi nodded. "According to the IPA code of leadership, any squad with more than seven people needs a second-in-command. Ever since we got Cago I've been considering between you and Zane. He studies strategy on his off time but you have seniority and better skills in combat. Besides, I didn't want to have any contention between the twins for one being over the other."

Flynn nodded. "Makes sense."

"Well Flynn," she asked, "will you take the position?"

He smiled. "It would be my honor."

Cago pulled his knife out, and watched the soldiers patrolling the wall. Reaching out, he used his abilities to spread a mist of darkness across the area in front of him.

Crouching low, he ran into the mist, knowing, almost in a sixth-sense kind of way, where everything was.

He ran unseen, cutting down soldier after soldier with ease. A short time later, they were all down.

"Well done," Zane's voice said as the simulation ended. After a moment, he exited the viewing room and walked into the area that Cago was in.

"You have done amazingly with your knife," Zane said. "However, Bi wants me to teach you with some more standard weapons." He tossed Cago a small gun. "We will start with this. All of the others, like you, have their specialities. Flynn is our main combat specialist, Tarff uses only his strength, Blackeye is long-range, Bi is our tactical, I am the pilot and programmer, and Ryan is the technician and heavy weapons specialist. Even though we do nearly perfect in these things, Cago, we have to learn how to fight in many different ways in order to survive."

Cago looked down at the gun in his hand. "What if this doesn't help me? What if it is easier with my knife?"

"If you survive all of these tests without the gun, I will allow you to bypass the rest of the gun training."

Zane turned and walked back into the viewing room, and he gave Cago a thumbs up. Cago shrugged back, and the simulation began.

14- Announcement

Marron Avenue, Long Beach
California, USA,
4:30 pm
Flynn

Flynn felt the wind blow past his face as he sprinted towards the burning house, hiveblade drawn. He and the rest of his squad were on an emergency support call from Clan Dax, and were now in Southern California.

The sun had almost begun to rise when Project 1672 had been attacked by Enforcement. Clan Dax had arrived quickly, but their forces were not strong enough to fight five platoons. So they called in all of Den Exon to help them.

"Scorpius!" Zane said through the intercom. "Five soldiers on your right." Flynn turned to see that he was correct. Flynn leapt towards them and cut through two at once as the others backed up. Seeing that their weapons did no damage, they began retreating farther down the street, towards the house. Quickly, Flynn pulled his shield off of his head and threw it towards them.

"Scorpius, behind you!" Zane called out.

Flynn spun to see a soldier with an A-15 turret, standing no less than ten feet away from him.

He quickly tried to summon his shield, but the soldier managed to hit him enough times to knock him off balance, and send him tumbling to the ground.

Flynn heard a yell from behind him as Tarff charged the turret, which tried in vain to shoot at the huge monstrosity before being crumpled into a pile of scraps. Tarff then ran over and picked up Flynn.

"What are you doing? I can still help," Flynn complained as Tarff carried him away.

"Check your arm."

Flynn looked down to find that his skin and suit on his right arm was completely shredded, and he could see his bone in multiple places. Because of the rush of the fight he had not felt it before, but the pain began to grow as the adrenaline wore off.

"Still think you can fight?" Tarff asked. After running past a full block of houses, Tarff turned and set him down on the roof of one, right next to where Blackeye was lying in a prone position, shooting towards the battle from hundreds of feet away. She looked up as Tarff arrived.

"Heal him," Tarff said.

Blackeye nodded and set down her rifle. She pressed her gloved hands down on Flynn's arm, and he watched as his wounds began to close. After a moment, she stopped and went back to shooting.

Flynn looked back down at his arm. The wound was still there, and looked pretty nasty, but was not nearly as bad as before.

"Thank you, Blackeye," Flynn said. She gave no indication that she heard him.

"Scorpius," Bi said through the intercom.

"Yes?"

"I want you to sit this one out," she said. "You are the only one here who has another assignment, and you are the one we need to keep safe."

"Affirmative Sergeant," Flynn said.

Flynn overlooked the battle. Enforcement troops were being depleted very fast, but they still had quite a bit left. An enemy chopper had crashed before Flynn had arrived, and two of the buggies were destroyed.

Flynn tried searching for his group members. Tarff wasn't hard to find, considering he was taller than all of the nearby homes. Ryan was pulling pieces of metal from around the area and forming them into various creature-shaped robots, which Zane would then spark to life amidst the attacking enemies, and Cago was nowhere to be found. He was probably invisible amidst the battle. After a few minutes, Flynn was able to locate some soldiers that were getting destroyed by what seemed to be an unseen force, which he assumed to be Cago.

"Project 1672 has safely been taken to safety," Bi said. "We have received orders to retreat."

Flynn waited for a few minutes before a Lander came to pick him up, along with Blackeye. The rest of the group awaited him inside.

"You got cut up pretty bad," Ryan said.

Flynn shrugged. "Blackeye helped a lot." He turned to Tarff. "Thanks for the support."

"Anytime," he said gruffly. "Man, I could really use a smoothie right now."

Ryan chuckled. "Is there ever a time that you don't want a smoothie?"

"Nope."

Ryan shook his head. "You're crazy."

"You guys are crazy," Tarff countered. "None of you even know how to do some proper cooking." No one could disagree. Tarff's cooking was amazing.

A while later, they pulled up to an office building, and they filed out of the vehicle.

"They need me in here for the status report," Bi said. "You guys will have to go in with Garret's squad."

"What about our Lander?" Tarff asked. "Aren't you going back with the officers?"

"Of course," she answered. "Flynn and Cago need this one. They have a party to go to."

The party. Flynn had almost forgotten about that. "That starts in four hours. It takes more than that just to get back to the warehouse."

"So it does," Bi replied. "You should have just enough time to get back and ready if Ryan's driving."

Ryan's jaw dropped. "You're letting me drive?" Ryan technically wasn't old enough to drive but he knew how to do it better than anyone else, even if his speeds at times could be... chaotic. They would be breaking the law by letting him drive but Flynn being alive was against the law so at this point they didn't care.

She tossed him the keys and smiled. "Don't look so surprised." She turned to Flynn. "Vilo has given you a task." She threw him a small black hexagonal disk. "They are worried about project 1711's safety. That is a tracking beacon. Your assignment is to put it on her." She paused and smiled. "Think you can get close enough to do that?"

He heard Cago cough violently into his fist behind him. "I'll try my best," Flynn said.

"Excellent," she said. "Ryan, try to be careful."

Ryan smiled, mocking Flynn. "I'll try my best."

Thanks to Ryan's driving, Flynn had gotten nearly a full hour of time to get ready, and yet he still felt like he looked bad when he met up with Emily. Of course she made *everyone* look bad, so he was even more worried about himself but, like always, she didn't seem to care.

Flynn had now been here, at Dom's house, for nearly another hour. Everyone was gathered in the main room, apparently waiting for Trevor to make his big announcement.

"Will everyone please quiet down!" Everyone stopped talking and looked up at Trevor, who was standing on a wooden stool near the kitchen. "All of you are probably wondering why I have gathered you here. Well, today is a very big day for my family. My dad's company has helped our community for years, and now, as of today, they are now working alongside Cadmore Industries!"

Surprised whispers filled the room.

"Right where we stand, we are supporting Enforcement soldiers all over the country! We-"

"Despite how much people say those robots are protecting us, they still freak me out," Emily whispered to Flynn. "I need some fresh air. Let's get out of here."

"Fresh air?" Flynn asked with a chuckle.

"Yup!" Emily smiled. "Ask Cago to come with us."

Flynn turned to his other side. “Cago, get Mia. We’re going.”

“I’m just supposed to tell her we are leaving?” Cago asked.

“Just say you need some fresh air.”

Cago turned and whispered something to Mia. She shrugged and followed after Emily and Flynn as they turned to leave.

“To the balcony?” Flynn asked.

“Sure,” Emily said. “Just away from there.” They walked up the stairs and out onto the deck, where they sat together on one couch, with Cago and Mia on the other.

“This is nice,” Emily said. “No fireworks, no people outside. It's just peaceful.”

Peaceful. That word was almost nonexistent to Flynn at this point in his life. Only a couple of hours ago, he had been shot at by a military-grade turret, and had had his arm torn open. Peaceful.

Flynn looked down at his arm. He had worn long sleeves to cover the wound, despite the warmth. Emily had asked him about it and he had said he was cold. She just shook her head and smiled.

“My grandpa used to teach me about all of the constellations,” Emily said. “Now every time I see a starry sky, I think of him." She sighed and leaned her head against his shoulder. Flynn smiled and put his arm around her. This may be peaceful for her, but Flynn felt like he was about to be ripped to pieces. And this time, there was no one shooting at him.

Flynn looked over at Cago, who was raising his eyebrows.

Oh, shut up, he mouthed.

Cago laughed, then his expression turned serious. *The bacon,* he mouthed.

The bacon?

Cago nodded and pointed towards Flynn's pocket. *Bacon.*

Flynn looked down at his pocket. The tracking beacon. He looked over at Emily, who was still lost in thought with her eyes closed.

Gently, Flynn used his powers to slide the small hexagon-shaped beacon out of his pocket and up towards his shoulder. Then, careful to not let his powers affect Emily, he moved the beacon above her neck.

Flynn watched as the small device scanned her smooth, semi-tan skin tone, then hovered slowly down until it rested on the back of her neck and turned invisible. He let out a sigh.

Emily turned towards him. "Do you ever wonder what they are doing out there? The IPA?"

Flynn shrugged. "I hear they are trying their best to fight for their species."

"Yeah," Emily said. "I've always heard that, but how do we know? And how are they fighting? The only thing I've heard of is the occasional outpost being destroyed or Enforcement patrol raid. The government almost makes them seem like terrorists."

"They aren't," Flynn said quickly.

Emily gave him a curious look. "I wasn't saying they were. I just said that is the way people make it seem."

"Oh." Flynn felt embarrassed. "What would you do if you were one of them?"

"I haven't ever thought about it," she said. "I guess I would just try my best to survive, or maybe find people who would support us."

"I suppose that would be good." Flynn thought about what she'd said. If she was an Ironborn, no one else would be able to recognize it. In fact, he wouldn't himself if he hadn't been saying similar things to try to hide his secret. It was kind of annoying sometimes that he had to hide who he truly was. He hated lying to Emily.

"Hey look! The Redstone," Emily said, and pointed up at the stars. Flynn looked where she was pointing. It was a constellation that consisted of three interlocking triangles.

"It is an old Indian constellation," she explained. "The Redstone is the most important of all the constellations in the religion that created it. It represents someone's passion. Their greatest driving source in life. It is also typically something that the person is willing to die to achieve."

"Interesting," Flynn said. Redstone was the name of the project that studied information about the Cadmore Industries war headquarters. Once the IPA found and destroyed it, they believed they would be able to win the war. There were definitely soldiers that died for such a cause.

Emily sighed again. "Aren't those two so cute together?" She pointed to Cago and Mia, who were talking on the other couch.

"I've never seen him so happy," Flynn said. "Nor have I seen him hold longer than a twenty-second conversation with a girl."

Emily smiled. "Were you much different before we met?"

Flynn laughed as he remembered the past. It was almost a year ago when he had met her. Five weeks from now would mark the date.

He chuckled again. "I was so strange back then."

"And you aren't now?" she asked.

"Nope," he said. "I'm even stranger."

Emily laughed. "Whatever you are, Flynn, it is far from strange."

Flynn shook his head. "You're oblivious."

"I am not!" She hit him on the arm. He was getting used to that.

"Then how come you haven't noticed how weird I am?" he asked.

She shrugged. "Maybe because *you're* oblivious."

"What is that supposed to mean?" he asked.

She smiled. "Nothing." She looked back up at the sky again. "What time is it anyway?"

Flynn reluctantly pulled his hand off of her shoulder and pulled back his sleeve to check his watch. "10:17"

He moved to put his arm back but before he did Emily stopped him. "Wait."

For a second Flynn froze. Had he done something to offend her? Did she not want his arm around her? He quickly prayed that the half-stick of deodorant he had put on had been enough.

She reached forward and pulled back the sleeve. She gasped and put her hand to her mouth. "Flynn, your arm!"

"Oh that?" he said, as he tried in vain to pull back down his sleeve. "It's nothing."

Emily couldn't take her eyes off the wound. "What happened?"

"I told you. Nothing." He tried again to pull down his sleeve, but she wouldn't let him.

"Did someone do this to you?" she asked.

"Of course not," Flynn answered. A robot had. "It was an accident."

She reluctantly pulled his sleeve back down to his wrist. "You should be in the hospital."

"Rather than here with you?" he said, as if it was absurd. "That would be crazy."

Emily shook her head. "You're already crazy."

"True," he said. He leaned back and put his arm around her shoulder. Luckily, this time, she seemed glad that it was there.

Flynn tried to see what she was thinking. Her posture, like always, was perfect. She was smiling softly, which meant she could be recalling a happy memory or... no, it was something else. Her eyes showed peacefulness, and were full of intelligence. Their dark blue color was darkened by the night sky, but were accented by the two lights behind them on the porch, giving them a deep, penetrating look. The light also reflected off of her hair, making it look silky as it fell down past her shoulders and cast a shadow on her soft, smooth skin. *Cut it out*, Flynn thought to himself. *You're trying to read her emotions, not study her beauty.*

Then again, Bi had warned him about this. You cannot read someone when you are distracted. "The ability to penetrate one's soul takes practice and complete concentration," she had once told him.

Well, it wasn't Flynn's choice to be distracted. Sure, he had tried to stop but he couldn't get himself to focus. Every time he tried, he just noticed something that made her even more perfect.

Flynn drew in a deep breath and closed his eyes. When he opened them, he looked back over to Emily, who was still staring up at the stars.

For a moment, Flynn saw something in her eyes, and guessed that she was thinking about her grandfather, as she always did when she saw stars. She had always told him stories about how close the two of them had been, and how much she missed him since he had died a little over a year ago.

He could almost see the stories she told. He saw them together, going on hikes through the moonlight, sitting outside and overlooking a lake as it reflected the stars, laughing and telling jokes, applauding her at every achievement she made, and finally, his death. It was not a sad memory. He had been old and prepared to pass on.

Emily reached up and pulled a strand of hair out of her face and tucked it behind her ear so it curled forwards. Flynn loved it when her hair did that. *Stop,* he told himself again.

Suddenly, Flynn heard a clanging noise downstairs. He turned towards Emily. "What was that?"

She shook her head. "I don't know." Her eyes were full of concern. Flynn hated when she was worried. She stood up. "Let's go see."

Cago and Mia, who also looked just as confused as Emily, stood up as the four of them opened the door, walking into the hallway and down the stairs.

When they came to the living room, everyone was applauding and cheering, but none of them could see why.

"Flynn, Cago, we have a Code 153. You need to get out of there." Flynn heard Zane's voice say. They always kept small comms in their ears, just in case they needed to know something.

Cago turned to Flynn and they both started to walk towards the back door, pushing their way through the crowd.

Emily ran up beside him. "Flynn, where are you going?"

"Sorry," he said. "My parents want me home."

"Do you have to leave now?" she asked.

"My parent's put a lot of trust in me coming here." Flynn said. "If I break that I might not be able to go to anything else like this."

"Yeah, I just..." she paused. "I guess I shouldn't pressure you to stay. I'll see you soon." She hugged him before turning to face Mia. Flynn's eyes lingered on her for a moment before turning back around and pushing through the crowd.

As they neared the back door, Flynn looked towards the kitchen and saw what everyone was cheering at. Standing not twenty feet away from the back door were two fully armored Enforcement soldiers.

Flynn guessed that they were only here for the grand announcement, but they were soldiers nonetheless.

Quickly, he and Cago crept to the back door. The movement must have caught one of the soldier's motion sensors, because it turned its head to gaze over at them. Flynn froze. Enforcement soldiers were built with machines to be able to detect an Ironborn using radiation sensors so they, in the past, would know who to defend in a battle. Now that they were against the same species, it proved useful for hunting them down.

Flynn tried to stay calm. An Ironborn's powers were linked with emotion. When they were drowsy, their powers were weak. When they had adrenaline, their power grew stronger and more noticable. Right now, Flynn had just been with Emily, which gave him tons of adrenaline, and was now face-to-face with an Enforcement officer, while surrounded by everyone who knew him. His radiation levels were probably skyrocketing right now.

The soldier slowly turned back to face the crowd, and Flynn let out a long breath as he kept moving towards the back door.

"We're very sorry." Flynn heard a voice that sounded a bit like Trevor's. Probably his dad. "The soldiers have gotten an important call they need to be on, and they need to leave immediately."

A loud, *Awwww,* came from the crowd.

Zane's voice crackled back in. "They've found you."

"Move!" Flynn whispered to Cago as he dragged him out the back door. The backyard only had a few people, mostly couples talking on the many benches around the massive lawn and garden areas.

Cago stuck his hands in his pockets and Flynn began to whistle as they slowly walked past them and waved to some of the people that looked up as they walked by. Finally, the two of them made it out of sight. Then they began sprinting away.

"Suits," Flynn said, and he engaged his suit as Cago did the same. He turned back to see that there was an Enforcement van parked in front of the house, and two more troops were standing outside of it. One was tall and broad and the other was small and agile. Two specialists. One recon. One officer. Almost had a full squad.

"There's one missing," Flynn mumbled.

"What?" Cago said.

"Get down!" Flynn shoved him to the side as a bullet struck the car that had been in front of him. The car that now had a three-foot hole in it. Flynn turned around to see a small figure on the roof of Dom's house, his mechanical hands loading another gigantic round into his sniper.

"Found him," Flynn said. Cago began to rise to his feet. "Cago, move to the backyards. They will beat us if we try to escape by road. Zane?"

"I'm on my way. Be on the lookout for the Rizen."

Flynn vaulted a fence and began running through someone's backyard. He could not see Cago, but could hear him running next to him. Flynn heard a loud crack as the fence they had just jumped over exploded into small splinters of wood by the sniper.

Flynn kept running as fast as he could.

"They have a second van," Ryan's voice chimed in. "They are going to try to cut you off."

Flynn used his powers to lower gravity as he jumped over the next fence, which was nearly ten feet high.

They ran through multiple backyards until coming out on another road. Flynn glanced over his shoulder to see the two reinforcement troops following behind. With the whole squad, this wouldn't have been a problem, but with just the two of them, it would be difficult. These were elites.

Flynn turned right and kept running. He had passed nearly a full block before a black Enforcement van pulled out of the road in front of him. Flynn turned back to the soldiers, weighing his options. Before he could decide, the Stealth soldier got tackled to the ground by an unseen force, and the Brute collapsed to the ground, a knife protruding from his abdomen.

"Nice," Flynn said to Cago.

The twosome ran away from the van. It was going fast, but the IPA suits made the humans much faster.

They were just beginning to get distance between them and the van when a second one appeared on the road in front of them. The soldiers in the first van piled out, making a wide circle around the two Ironborn, guns raised.

Flynn pulled out his mataka and hiveblade. They were hopelessly outnumbered. They didn't stand a chance. The soldiers stood ready for a moment, and Flynn braced for them to fire. It never came.

A human Enforcement officer in a black uniform stepped out of the second van. "Excellent." He walked through the ring of soldiers. "This is a good capture. These two are very strong for their size."

Capture? Why hadn't they tried to kill them yet?

"I see you are confused about why you are not yet dead," the man said. Now that he was closer, Flynn could see that he was tall and thin, sporting a black goatee. He looked like an actor from an FBI show. "Well, I cannot tell you without being killed myself, but you should count yourselves as lucky. You now have a chance to live." He turned to the robots. "Restrain them."

Two soldiers walked forward, each holding a set of large black handcuffs. To hold a superhuman, they didn't look like much, but Flynn knew that they were designed to do just that, and he had seen them in action before.

Flynn was beginning to think about how he could get away from this, when one of the approaching soldiers dropped to the ground, a gaping hole in his chest.

The other soldiers looked around frantically, searching for the source of the attack. Then the second soldier collapsed. The human officer ran back to the van and opened the door. He got inside and began talking loudly into his radio. Before he could get anything out however, the officer slumped over, a bullet wound in his head. Then the van exploded.

Flynn heard a loud humming noise and looked up to see the Rizen overhead, gunning down both vans and all of the enemy soldiers that were surrounding the twosome.

"Man, I love that ship," Flynn said.

It lowered itself down near the ground, and Flynn jumped inside the already-open hatch, Cago following close behind. They passed Blackeye, who had three missing bullets from her belt. She had been the one who had shot the officer and the soldiers that were trying to handcuff them.

"Thank you," Flynn said.

She just nodded.

Flynn ran to the front of the ship as it began taking off. Zane was sitting in the front seat of the cockpit, with Ryan next to him. "Sorry I couldn't come quicker," he said.

"We tried to get here faster," Ryan said,

"But we got into a situation."

"They had a chopper waiting for us."

"Along with a ground squad."

"I didn't seem like they were trying to stop us."

"Just stall for long enough-"

"To get you killed," Ryan finished.

"Although it didn't seem as if they were trying to kill you," Zane said.

"Yeah," Ryan agreed.

"They didn't," Flynn said. "The officer said that he was going to capture us."

"Strange," they said at the same time.

"I'm going to tell Bi about it," Flynn said. "She will know what to do."

"Did you see me take out all of those soldiers?" Ryan asked. "It only took me seconds and all of them were gone." He mimicked himself using the Rizen's turret.

"Well, you couldn't have done it without my expert flying skills," Zane said.

"Oh yeah?" Ryan and Zane leapt into a debate about who was the greater help in the battle as they flew back to the warehouse. Flynn would have been scared of someone seeing the vehicle, but he knew it could turn nearly invisible.

They pulled into the garage and walked down the ramp to the warehouse floor.

"Welcome home, soldiers," Proxy said in her robotic voice as they came inside.

Bi approached them. "What happened?"

Flynn shook his head. “Something very strange.” He began explaining the story, excluding only the parts with Emily. Cago added in small snippets here and there.

“Strange indeed,” Bi said. They had safely made it back to the warehouse, and had told Bi about the situation. Even though it was well past midnight, she was still awake. “Vilo and the den lieutenants have heard of this happening of late. And not only in our clan. Instead of killing the Ironborn, they are taking them into custody.”

“So this isn’t new?” Cago asked.

“This is definitely new,” Bi said. “Disappearances have been going on for a while. You, however, are the first to have survived the incident. I will speak to Vilo about this. Thank you, Flynn and Cago. This could prove to be very valuable information.”

The firestorm comes to you Flynn. The trial of a lifetime is nearly at hand.

Flynn woke up. He pulled off the covers, feeling the sweat that now drenched his night clothes. He walked across his room to his dresser and looked at the three pictures currently sitting there. The first, the picture of Split with Nebula. The second, a picture of him beside his parents, all three of them smiling happily. His mother had never taken the normal “smiling” pictures, where everyone was just sitting, looking at the camera. Their family pictures were never scheduled. They were always just shots of them having a good time. Playing together, laughing, the real moments he wanted to remember. Finally, he looked at the last picture. It was taken from a school yearbook in 8th grade. It showed Flynn, along with Cago, doing a group project in science at the beginning of the school year. Seated across from him was Emily. The three of them were all laughing while telling jokes to each other while doing the project, which had been about bird nesting on page fourteen of their packets. That had been the first day he had met Emily, and he had never forgotten a single second of it.

"I wish you could meet her, mom." Flynn smiled. "You would love her."

He heard a light creaking noise in the hallway behind him. Curious, he went to his door and peeked outside. He looked left and right. There was nothing.

Then, he heard another noise down the hallway to his right. Footsteps. Exiting his room, Flynn followed the footsteps away from the stairs and past the last bedroom. There was now a door in front of him. The door to the roof.

Flynn opened it and climbed the ladder, pushing open the trapdoor at the top silently. He then climbed out and closed it.

Sitting on the edge of the roof, looking out over the forest, was Cago, wearing his usual black jeans with a black jacket, holding his knife in his hand.

“What are you doing up here, Cago?” he asked, walking toward where he was seated.

“This is a nice view,” Cago said. He seemed to be lost in thought.

“Yeah, it’s also a pretty big fall,” Flynn said. “Do you think that you could view it from a safer angle?”

Cago took a deep breath. “I like knowing that there is an edge, Flynn. Even if I know I’ll never use it, it’s nice to know that it’s there. That there is a way to leave everything behind, to move on.”

Flynn looked over at him, trying to read what he was thinking.

“I’ve tried it before you know,” he said. “Killing myself. I’ve tried to do it.” He began flipping his knife and then catching it in his hand. “The first time was the night when my brother died. Jordan and I looked nothing alike. He had black skin and was tall and strong, like my father. I am pale, skinny and Asian, like my mother. But he didn’t care about our differences. We were brothers. He, like me, was an Ironborn. Of course, my dad didn’t know this, considering he was the leader of a gang that killed Ironborn, but Jordan had powers. In fact, my brother was actually part of my father’s gang for a while. He was forced into it. But that was before he died. It was the very first night of the Purge. He might have even been the first Ironborn to be killed by Enforcement when they turned. That night, I went to the top of the TRA building.”

"The TRA building?" Flynn asked. "But that's more than twenty-five stories tall."

"How did you know that?" Cago asked.

"My mom used to work there," Flynn said.

"Oh," Cago said. "Well, I sat at the top, overlooking the city for about four hours. Then, I jumped off. I fell more than two hundred feet, and somehow, when I hit the ground, nothing happened. I stood up and walked away unharmed.

"The next time was about a year later. You, Jackson and Dom always say that I should try to talk to people more but I have never told you guys why I don't. That day, I had built up all the courage I could to go talk to a girl in one of my classes. I was stressing all day about how she would react. When I went over to say something, she shut me down. She looked at me like I was a creep and then walked away. I was feeling really bad as I left the school, and when I got home, my mom and dad were in an argument. Again. I went up into my room and listened to them yelling for hours and my anger just built up more and more. When I finally went downstairs, my emotions were built up too strong, and my powers manifested themselves for the first time. My father would never kill his own son like he would the rest of the Ironborn, but he could not live with one. So he left.

"That night, I was walking down the road, trying to think about what had just happened and I saw a truck coming. I didn't even really think about it. I just stepped out onto the road." He moved some of the hair out of his eyes. "But when it hit me, I didn't die. I didn't get mangled like you would expect. I just got thrown backward a few feet and stood up with some scratches on my elbows. The strangest part was, the truck was in much worse condition than I was. The whole front had been bent in and destroyed.

"The last time was when my mom died. She didn't just die from a normal cause, Flynn. She died on the night of a full moon." He swallowed. "I didn't know that the werewolf effect even existed at that point. I used my powers and next thing I know I'm waking up to my house on fire and my mom dead. My aunt tried to help me learn how to control myself when using my powers on those nights but...now she's dead too." He paused. "I just couldn't handle it anymore. First my brother, then my dad, and now my mom. I went into her closet and pulled out the gun that she always kept in case she was in danger. The gun that she didn't use on me.

"I had the gun in front of my heart and pulled the trigger. The bullet stopped in the barrel. It took me a moment to realize that the thing that had stopped it was my knife, which was hanging around my neck. That is when I started to piece things together. The fact that my knife never dulled, never chipped, never rusted, and now it had stopped a bullet, I began to realize what was going on. My knife had been the first thing to hit the ground when I jumped off of the TRA building. My knife was the first thing that had hit the semi when I walked out into the street. I have always felt like my knife wasn't just a piece of metal. It has always seemed like a part of me, like an extension of my body. It has saved my life many times from people trying to hurt me. And that includes myself."

Flynn paused, trying to understand what he was saying. "So your knife has its own mind?"

"I don't know," Cago said. "Somehow Bi figured out that it wasn't an ordinary knife and I let her look at it. She has no idea what it is. She even ran it under a scanner and it couldn't tell her what metal it was. The scanner just said 'Error' and then the screen blanked out."

"Well Cago, we should both get some rest." Flynn rubbed his chin. "If it gives you peace to know that there is a way out, that's fine. Just promise me you won't use it."

For the first time, Cago looked back at him. "I'll try."

15- Red Army

Domonic's House, Sacramento
California, U.S.A
2:15 p.m.
Flynn

Flynn was failing. His muscles were straining and he could feel them giving out but he couldn't let them. This was a matter of life and death and he wasn't about to give up.

Well, it was a matter of ten dollars, but Flynn still wasn't going to surrender.

Jackson grunted, struggling in vain to push Flynn's hand onto the table.

"Today we will finally find out," Dom said. "Flynn versus Jackson. The battle of all battles."

The trio was back at Dom's house once again. They had been here for a few hours and were helping Dom's parents clean up everything from the night before. Well, they *had* been helping. Right now Flynn and Jackson were currently locked in an arm wrestle, and Jackson had bet ten bucks that he could win. Little did he know that Flynn wasn't even trying.

Jackson's face was contorted as his muscles strained against Flynn's. "Oh, you are so beat, Jackson," Dom taunted. "Come on Flynn!"

Flynn raised an eyebrow at Jackson. "Is this all you got?"

Jackson tried harder but there was nothing he could do. Flynn was much stronger than he let on. He had to be careful though, otherwise his friends might start getting suspicions.

Pretending to struggle, Flynn slowly overpowered Jackson, getting his hand nearly to the breaking point before his friend gave up and his hand slammed down onto the table.

Dom and Flynn cheered as Jackson handed them ten dollars each. "That game was rigged," Jackson complained.

Flynn chuckled in his mind as he realized that, technically, it was. "I'm sure it was." He patted Jackson's shoulder.

The sound of footsteps drew their attention to Dom's mom as she walked into the room. "Time for your friends to go, Dom. You need to go to soccer practice."

"Fine," Dom sighed. "See you guys later, I guess."

Jackson stood up from the table and followed Flynn over to the front door. "Do you need a ride back home?" he asked.

"You know," Flynn tried to stay casual. The less his friends knew about where he lived the better. "I think I'll walk home today."

"Fine with me," Jackson said. As they walked down the pathway to the sidewalk a car pulled up in front of the house and Jackson hopped inside before being driven away.

Flynn exhaled as he looked east, preparing for the miles ahead. "Here we go," he said, and began to slowly make his way up the street.

As he walked, his thoughts instantly turned to the war. Why did he always do that? His mind was always thinking about it, always strategizing. He supposed that, while they were currently at war, having his mind always sharp was good but sometimes he wished he could have a moment when he didn't have to worry about any of that stuff. But he couldn't. The risk of getting caught off guard was too high.

The only new information that Flynn's squad had gotten from the IPA was about a mission from Clan Xion, but they seemed to have everything under control. Flynn, along with the others, were getting anxious. Something was coming, and there was no knowing when.

Flynn turned the corner at the end of the street, which led him in front of the highschool. He looked at it for a moment, remembering all the good memories he had had there.

Unlike nearly everyone he knew, Flynn actually enjoyed school. It was a nice break from all the fighting. A time of peace. And Emily being there was obviously a big plus.

It was strange to remember the time when he met her. For the first few months the two of them had just been friends, and there was never even a thought in his mind of ever liking her. Obviously those thoughts had changed, but it had taken a while for her to grow on him. It was only then that he saw how beautiful and amazing she was. He thought that was how it ought to be. They were friends first, and they always would be.

Then, of course, there were his other friends. Jackson and Dom. To be honest, Flynn didn't even know how they had survived all of the reckless things they had done together. Flynn himself had felt in danger multiple times and brushing off injuries was much easier for him than any regular human.

He remembered back to the time when they had successfully leapt onto a moving train down by the station. How fast the train had been going when they got on, well... that didn't matter. What mattered was that they had done it.

Flynn's thoughts were cut off as his instincts acted up. He could see a flicker of movement in the reflection of a window on the school. Three teenage boys, approaching him from down the road, walking quickly. As Flynn got a closer look, he could see that the middle boy was Trevor and he was mad.

Not wanting to make a scene, Flynn decided to turn down a side road into a neighborhood. Trevor followed. The fact that he followed into the neighborhood meant that he wasn't going to give up. If Flynn couldn't lose him, he needed to get him to a place where they wouldn't attract attention.

Flynn walked past another few houses before turning onto a paved biking path. Luckily for him, the path had a wall on either side, blocking the whole area from view of the houses. Perfect.

"Hey Flynn!" Flynn spun, as if noticing Trevor for the first time. He and his two comrades had just entered the path, but were walking quickly. "We need to talk to you about your friend."

Flynn waited until they were a few feet away from him. "My friend?"

"Yes." Trevor said, trying to put on an intimidating look. To any regular person it would have worked. Trevor was tall, muscular and had a reputation for beating people up for being in his way. Flynn, however, wasn't worried in the slightest.

"Your friend took my date," Trevor accused.

"Actually your date took my friend," Flynn said, putting his hands into the pockets of his leather jacket. "Must say it was quite a lonely evening for me."

"Don't play smart with me." Trevor brushed a piece of his long blonde hair out of his face. "Your friend is going to pay for this."

"How much does he owe you?" Flynn asked, still casual. "I've heard his parents are loaded."

"Nothing." Trevor smiled darkly, still angry. "We just need to *talk* to him." The other two boys chuckled.

"Oh, well, I'm sure I could tell him for you," Flynn said. "It would save a whole lot of time."

"You want to deliver the message for us?" Trevor asked.

"Sure."

"Alright," Trevor said. Swinging his arm around, Trevor punched Flynn in the face. Flynn pretended to take it worse than he did, falling down on one knee. "Give that to your friend for us, will you?" Trevor's two friends laughed again.

"That's all?" Flynn stood up and shook himself a bit as if he was hurt. "I'm not even sure I could punch him that soft if I tried."

The smile faded from Trevor's face as he punched Flynn again, going for the gut this time.

Flynn stumbled back, even though he didn't feel a thing.

"Then maybe I'll have to tell him myself," Trevor said, grabbing Flynn's shoulders and throwing him onto the pavement. "Or perhaps that wouldn't hurt enough." He went for a kick in the ribs and Flynn groaned, rolling onto his side. "Maybe I'll just deliver the message to your girlfriend."

Trevor swung for another punch at Flynn's face but this time the punch had no effect, his fist stopping right at as it connected.

Flynn didn't even flinch. "Now you've crossed the line."

With a single punch from Flynn, Trevor was on the ground in the fetal position, a hand holding his jaw.

His two friends rushed forwards but Flynn simply dodged to the side, tripping the one on the left and kneeing him in the face as he fell to the ground.

As the other friend ran past him, Flynn kicked the back of his knee, sending him to the floor.

"Now that was just too easy," Flynn said, dusting his hands off.

The three boys stood up, backing away from Flynn. "Your friend will still pay for this," Trevor said.

"Sure he will," Flynn called after them as they ran away.

Flynn chuckled and shook his head as he continued down the path. Trevor deserved it. He had beaten up so many people without consequence, all because his father was the football coach. He needed someone to stand up to him.

And that was what the IPA was all about. Standing up for those who couldn't defend themselves. Putting your life on the line in an act of courage to protect freedom and equality. Flynn just wished more people could see that the Ironborn weren't bad. Sure, they weren't perfect, but neither was anyone else. They were just like humans, and should be treated as such.

As Flynn walked off of the path and back onto the sidewalk, his senses perked up again, as if his brain was trying to tell him something was coming. This happened often to Flynn, but normally he would be able to tell what it was that he needed to notice. As he looked around, he saw nothing.

Shrugging, he continued down the road. It was about four more miles back to the warehouse.

"Hey Flynn!"

Flynn sighed. "Not again." But as he turned around he was surprised to see a car pulling up beside him. The driver seat window was rolled down and Flynn could see Emily sitting behind the wheel, her mom next to her.

"Hey Emily!" he said. "What's up?"

"Me and my mom were just driving to get my hours in for my permit and we were wondering if you needed some help," she said.

"Help with what?"

"Um." She pointed. "Your eye?"

Confused, Flynn felt the area around his eye. When he pulled his hand away it was covered in blood.

He chuckled. "I didn't even notice."

"What happened to you?" Emily's mom asked from the passenger seat. Emily's mother Janelle was the nicest person that Flynn had ever met. She treated everyone like one of her own kids.

"I just tripped," Flynn responded offhandedly.

"Oh no," Janelle accused. "That wound was done by another person. I served as a nurse in the military for eight years, boy. I know a punch when I see one. Get in the car. I'm going to patch you up."

"I'm fine, really. I just need to-"

"No, no, stop arguing," she said. "I've got a first aid kit at home and I can get you right and-"

"I'm not getting out of this, am I?" Flynn asked Emily as her mother continued to ramble.

Emily smiled. "Nope."

Flynn sighed as he opened the door and hopped into the car. As he closed the door he was quickly handed a wad of tissues.

"Put this over the cut. It'll hold back the bleeding."

"Thanks Janelle," Flynn said, holding the tissues against the wound. In the rear view mirror he could see that the cut was about two inches in length and jagged, with a purple spot beginning to form around it. This meant it was the sidewalk that had cut him, and all the punch had done was give him a small bruise.

"So you're finally going to get your permit, huh?" Flynn asked Emily jokingly.

"You don't have to say it like that," Emily replied. She had always been scared of driving. "I'm not *that* late."

"I don't know," Flynn said. "Eight months seems a little late to me."

"I'm just glad she's going to be able to drive soon," Janelle said. "Then she can go to the grocery store for me." They all chuckled.

As Emily and her mother started talking to each other, Flynn sat back in his seat. He always found it odd seeing people like this. Talking and joking around with their family. It had only been three years since he lost his family and yet he barely remembered it at all. He sometimes wondered why he didn't miss having a family. Was the idea so foreign to him that he didn't know what he was missing out on? Flynn didn't know. And he probably never would. In fact, Flynn had always wondered what he was going to do after the war ended. Where would he go?

"We're here," Janelle said, cutting off Flynn's thoughts.

The three of them hopped out of the car as Janelle rushed inside as if Flynn was in critical condition. She was so caring for everyone else. So selfless.

Bi was a different sort of caring. More like a mentor and a teacher than a parent. That, of course, was good when you were at war, but sometimes Flynn wondered what she was like outside of the war. If all the guns and fighting had never been in her life, would she be more soft? Not that Bi was very hard on him, it was just weird to think of anyone in his squad without associating them with war. Flynn couldn't tell if that was good or really sad.

Emily led Flynn inside where Janelle sat him down on the couch. She cleaned up his wound with some chemicals before handing a bandage to Emily. "Can you bandage him up?" she asked. "I have to go put something in the oven."

"Sure," she replied.

After Jannelle left the room Flynn turned to Emily. "I really don't need it."

"My mom won't let you leave without it," she said with a smile.

"Fine," Flynn said as she put the bandage over his cut.

"So who punched you?" Emily inquired.

Flynn hesitated. "Just some guys from school."

Emily tilted her head to the side, overlooking the bandage. "Trevor?"

"I didn't say that," Flynn responded.

She smiled knowingly. "Mia told me that Trevor was mad at Cago."

Flynn said nothing.

"It's so sad that people dislike him," she said, sitting on the couch beside Flynn. "Cago's really nice if you take the time to get to know him. People just think he's weird because he's different. I mean, who said different was bad?"

"Most of the world right now, apparently," Flynn replied.

"What do you mean by that?" Emily asked.

"Well..." Flynn thought for a second. "There are plenty of people that are just as amazing as anyone else but are just seen as bad because people don't know who they really are."

Emily sat for a long time, looking into Flynn's eyes as if she was studying them.

"What?" he eventually asked.

"There's something else, isn't there?"

Flynn was silent, unsure of what to say.

After a few seconds, she grabbed his hand. "Come here."

Flynn followed as she led him back into her room. She walked over to her desk and opened her computer. Flynn sat on the edge of her bed for a few seconds as she searched for a website.

"Look at this," she said, beckoning him over. He stood up and looked over her shoulder at the computer screen. On her screen was a page with the words "Red Army" at the top, followed by a symbol consisting of three interlocking triangles.

The Ironborn from the IPA and the humans in the Red Army had worked side by side for years now, and although Flynn had not had much direct contact with them, he knew that they existed. He also knew that the Red Stone project, which was the hunt for Cadmore Industries headquarters, was named after the same thing that the Red Army was.

"What is it?" he asked, pretending to be confused.

"The Red Army is an underground group of human Ironborn supporters," Emily said. "Their name comes from the Red Stone. Remember the constellation that I told you about?"

"The one your grandfather would tell you about?"

She paused. "Well, I actually learned about that from this document. I didn't mean to lie to you I just wanted to see if you would recognize-" She stopped. "That isn't important. What's important is that there are others like us, Flynn. Others that believe in fulfilling the dream of having equality for all people." She turned to him, her bright eyes filled with both nervousness and hope. "You are one of us, right? One of the people who believe that the Ironborn aren't evil?"

Flynn didn't know how he should respond. Even now that he knew she was one of the supporters, he couldn't tell her that he was Ironborn. It was too risky. But could he tell her that he was a supporter of them?

"Flynn?" she asked. Her voice almost sounded scared.

Flynn nodded. "I think that everyone should be equal. Despite what people have said, I've never personally seen them do anything wrong, so I don't know why they should be treated unfairly."

She smiled excitedly and stood up. "I knew it!" She gave him a hug. "Gosh, this is such a relief."

Flynn smiled. "It's nice to know that there are more of us out there."

She sat down on her bed. "All the hate behind them doesn't make sense. There's so much propaganda and blaming without evidence to go with it. Until I have my own experience, I'm willing to believe that they are just like the rest of us."

The two of them held each other's eyes for a moment, just sitting in the silence.

"You should probably get out of here before my mom starts offering you food," she said. "Dinner is almost ready and you'll never be able to leave once she asks you if you're hungry."

Flynn laughed. "I bet." He stood up and walked out of the room, Emily following behind after quickly shutting down her computer.

As he packed up his things, Flynn studied Emily's actions. Her claiming to be a human supporter did not eliminate the possibility of her being Ironborn. Or did it? Flynn would have to speak to Bi on the subject.

Flynn thanked Janelle before walking out the door. As he continued down the street, he glanced back at

Emily's house. "Never be able to leave," he chuckled. "Doesn't sound so bad to me."

16- Discoveries

Sacramento
California, U.S.A
3:30 p.m.
Flynn

"You did what?" Bi exclaimed.

"We joined the Red Army," Flynn explained again.

"I know what you did." Bi shook her head in disbelief. "I am just surprised." A few minutes after leaving Emily's house Flynn had gotten a phone call from Bi asking if he wanted a ride, and they were currently driving in the Lamborghini back towards the warehouse. "I have heard of the Red Army before. It is known throughout the IPA, and we have many hidden contacts within it. I myself am a part of it. How did you find out she was a member?"

"Well," Flynn explained, "up until today I didn't even know that she thought the Ironborn were good."

"She doesn't know you have powers does she?" Bi asked.

"No," Flynn answered. "She doesn't know enough about the Ironborn for me to trust her that much. Sometimes I wonder what her reaction would be if I told her."

"Well we shouldn't try to find out," Bi said. "No matter how much you trust her, Flynn, you need to keep it a secret. For your own safety."

"Agreed." As much as Flynn hated to keep secrets, especially from Emily, Bi was right. Anyone could be a spy.

Flynn looked out the window and watched the trees and buildings as they zoomed past the highway. School was going to start soon. The pivotal point of a war was at hand. Flynn could die at nearly any second, and all he could think about was a girl. Sometimes he believed his brain was going to get him killed one day.

Suddenly something out the window caught his eye. He turned and looked behind the car. They had just passed the place where they would normally turn to go to the warehouse. He turned to Bi and was about to ask but she answered him first. "We are going to a meeting, Flynn."

"What?" Flynn exclaimed. "Why didn't you tell me?"

Bi smiled. "I didn't want you to be stressed."

He began to calm down, trusting his sargeant's choices.

"Besides," she continued. "I only found out a few minutes ago." She pulled off the highway and into an office parking lot. They both got out of the car and walked inside. The receptionist smiled as they entered.

"What can I help you with today?" he asked.

"I'm here for a board meeting," Bi smiled.

"Which one?" he asked.

She pulled out a card from her pocket and handed it to him. He looked down at it, then back up at her. "I see. Up the stairs and to your left."

"Thank you." Bi and Flynn began to follow his directions. She began to put the card back in her pocket when Flynn realized that he recognized the symbol on it.

"Isn't that the Redstone?" He pointed at the card.

She pulled it out. "Yes." She looked at him curiously. "How did you know that? I didn't know you studied constellations."

"Emily showed me it a few weeks ago," he explained.

"Oh," she said. "I guess that makes sense. The Redstone is the symbol of the Red Army, hence its name."

They both stopped in front of a set of double wooden doors. "Flynn, I expect they will ask about your situation with the Enforcement officer. You need to tell them everything. Are you ready?"

Flynn nodded, and she opened the door.

The room was dim, and had a long table seated with many people, all of them wearing their clan suits. This meant that they were waiting for his arrival. Flynn wasn't allowed to know who they were for safety reasons.

"Welcome Flynn," Vilo said. He could recognize her because of her suit design. The design of a captain. It also had red highlights, the color of Clan Vilo, and a captain's badge on her shoulder plate, also marked with red. "We have some questions for you." She gestured to a seat and he sat down. "Please describe to us your encounter with the Enforcement officer."

He described the situation to her in the best detail he could, excluding the parts beforehand with Emily. Some of the den lieutenants scribbled down notes or asked questions as he went.

"The Enforcement officer in question is named Admiral Fox," Bi said after he was finished.

"And he perished?" Vilo asked curiously.

"He was shot by one of my own soldiers," Bi said.

"Admiral Fox is a high ranking human Industry officer. His death is a great victory, but his appearance is concerning," Vilo said. "Thank you, Flynn. We will have to discuss this further." When she said nothing more Flynn understood that that was his cue to leave. Bi tossed him the keys, and he exited the office to go wait in the car.

He walked briskly down the hall and the stairway, pushing out of the front doors and walking over to the Lamborghini. From the outside, it looked like an ordinary luxury sedan, but Flynn knew that Ryan and Zane had added in many upgrades, weapons, and armor, along with connecting it to Proxy. The twins had always called it their car, not because they could legally drive it, but because they had built it. They built a lot of things around the warehouse.

When he got to the car, he pulled out the keys to unlock it, and realized they were the wrong ones. The Lamborghini's key was electric, but these were just normal metal keys. Flynn recognized them as the keys to the truck.

He turned back towards the building. This was not a mistake that Bi would ever overlook. Not only that, the keys of the truck weren't even supposed to be here. Because the truck stayed in the warehouse garage all day, they just left the keys in the ignition.

Then again, Bi always has reasons for what she does, Flynn thought. *There has to be some reason for this.*

He began slowly walking back to the building, pushing open the door and walking back up the stairs. He got to the door and was about to knock when something he heard caught his attention.

"Agent Scorpius does not have the skill level to do this." It was Bi's voice. Why was she talking about him?

"He clearly does, considering he has already completed the assignment." Vilo. Could she be talking about Emily?

Bi spoke up again. "And the aftermath? He is not ready for-"

"Death is part of war," Vilo said. "If your soldiers aren't strong enough to watch loved ones die then they are a weak link in the chain of our organization, and should therefore should be considered as such." Death? Flynn began to get worried. "People have been disappearing everywhere. Are their lives less significant than hers?" Hers. It was a girl.

"It is one thing to give a soldier the risk of dying on the battlefield while protecting himself," Bi responded. "It is very different to give a soldier, especially a junior, the task to turn a friend into a tool. A piece of bait waiting to be eaten and destroyed. I agree with the fact that the information would prove very valuable, but it is not worth the risk. Scorpius is my best soldier, and has possibly the best morale of them all, but I don't think even he can handle this."

"Then follow the extraction plan and don't tell him about it," Vilo replied.

"Tell him it was an accident?" Bi exclaimed. "Lie to him and say that it was unexpected for Project 1711 to get captured and possibly killed when we really set it up the whole time? I refuse. He needs to know."

"You do realize that by denying the orders of a higher ranking officer that you are risking being deleted, don't you?" Vilo asked.

"Who are you going to make the next sergeant if I am gone?" Bi asked. "Blackeye has the most experience, but is not fit to be a leader. Flynn would be next, but he is ruled out for obvious reasons. After that is Tarff, our heavyweight, who is intelligent, but overestimates his team member's abilities. Who then? Zane or Ryan? They don't have nearly enough experience. Cago has none. By removing me, you are rendering my squad leaderless."

"I could take it." Flynn had heard that voice a few times before. It was his den leader, Lieutenant Exon.

"There is no need for a lieutenant," Vilo said flatly. "Bi, you have a point, but it is invalid. If you are unable to follow orders, your squad will be broken up."

There was silence for a few moments.

"Very well. Is there anything else our squad needs to do?" Bi asked.

Vilo paused. "Lieutenant Quark, have you gotten the signal yet?"

"Yes," a voice answered. "Negative. They are not in need of assistance."

"Well then Bi," Vilo said. "For the time being, just more research and preparation."

Bi hesitated, as if she wanted to continue the discussion, but complied. "Yes captain."

Finally, Flynn knocked on the door. He heard the quiet whirring and clicking sound of many helmets going on. "You may enter," Vilo's voice said. Flynn walked through the door.

"What are you doing?" Bi asked.

"You um... gave me the wrong keys." He could feel the eyes of the officers seated around the table boring into him.

"Oh." Bi paused. "So I did." They quickly exchanged keys. "I will only be a few more minutes."

Flynn exited the office and started down the hallway. It wasn't until he had made it to the car, sat down and closed the door, that he began to process what he had just heard.

The whole reasoning behind Project 1711 had been a lie. He had not been sent to study her to see if she had abilities. He had not been sent to place a tracking beacon on her so they could know where she was when the Industry attacked. No, he had been sent to place a tracking beacon on her so they would know where she went after she got captured. They were using her as bait. As a pawn that needs to die in order to checkmate the king. Flynn felt like he wanted to punch a hole through the car, but decided against it because it wouldn't solve anything, and he probably couldn't do it anyways considering how armored the IPA's vehicles were.

"The Extraction Plan" Vilo had called it. Such a cruel name for such a cruel idea.

Flynn leaned back in his seat. Bi must have known he would come. She had wanted him to hear it. She couldn't do anything about it without losing her whole squad, but she was now trusting that *he* would. And he wasn't going to let her down.

17- Something Not So Peaceful

The Warehouse, Sacramento
California, U.S.A
4:30 p.m.
Flynn

Flynn sat cross-legged on a plush stool, looking forward at Bi, who sat in front of him, her hair in its usual messy afro. This was one of Flynn's favorite parts of the day. Bi's intellectual lessons.

"There are three main sections to social strategy," she began. "The first is the perceiver's tactic. This is the ability to be able to read what people are thinking without them telling you. A perceiver will instead study their enemy's body language and voice tones. They can then infer how they think their enemy would react to things based on how they have assessed them. This can be useful during conflict. A person with the perceiver's tactic can guess his enemy's next move." She paused for a moment. "The second is the convincer's tactic. Convincers are your social butterflies who are also good at convincing people to do things. Flynn, I ask you, what is the best way to get someone to tell you something?"

Flynn considered her question for a moment. "Normally you can act as if you don't care about a subject and then slowly put more strain on it until they break."

"That is part of it," she agreed. "Let me ask you something." She pulled a paperclip out of her pocket. "How much would you be willing to trade for this?"

Flynn shrugged. "Typically, maybe a few cents, unless I believe it has more value for some reason."

"Exactly," Bi stated. "Let's say that, hypothetically, this paperclip was dropped by a man that fled the scene of a murder."

"Then its value goes up."

"Exactly," Bi said. "But it can go a level deeper. If I really wanted to get a lot out of this paperclip, and you would believe anything I said, I would go with something more personal. Just for the lack of a better example, let's say that the person murdered was Emily. And this was the only thing the murderer dropped."

Flynn stopped. "Then I would do nearly anything to get it."

"Precisely," Bi said. "The same goes with information. I can make a piece of information seem much more valuable than it already is." She shifted slightly on her stool. "There is another tactic that convincers use. Let's say that, as an imposter, I was trying to get you to tell me an important detail about your father's death. I could first try to comfort you from the experience, but that might not do very much. However, if I were to share a similar experience about my own father's tragic death, it might get you closer to telling me what I want to know. It is empathy instead of sympathy. People are more comfortable talking to someone who seems just as vulnerable as they feel. You must drop to your enemy's level."

"I guess that makes sense," Flynn responded.

"Good," Bi continued. "The last ability is the solver's tactic. The solver is an expert thinker. Like the perceiver, they find every single possibility. They notice every detail. But this ability does not enable you to be able to get something from someone. Instead, it enables you to combat the enemy's intellect." She paused. "Let's say that again, I was trying to get the information out of you about your father's death. If you were a solver, you would be able to figure out that I am trying to pry the information from you, and then be able to checkmate me."

"Like chess?" Flynn asked.

"Yes. Very similar actually," Bi said. "You see, in chess, you can threaten the king multiple times before succeeding in winning the match. In intellectual combat, you will need to find chinks in their armor. Threaten them a few times. In intellectual combat, you need to threaten them a few times as well. Find the chinks in *their* armor. Eventually they will get caught in their own web, and the truth will come out on top. Make sense?"

"I think I'm getting the hang of it," Flynn answered.

"Good," Bi smiled. "This lesson is now adjourned. I need to go check up on Cago's training."

"Alright," Flynn said, and stood up to leave, Bi following behind. "How far has he gotten?"

"He has gotten to training level 22 in section D, but hasn't gotten higher than 10 in any of the others. His skill with a knife is almost good enough to challenge your hiveblade skills, but his aim with long-range weapons is horrific."

Flynn chuckled. "Even after his first real fight, he still doesn't understand that they are a necessity."

"He is very connected to that knife," Bi said. "Hasn't let it out of his sight since his dad left." They walked in silence for a while until they reached the door to Flynn's room.

"What are you going to do?" Bi asked.

"Probably more training," Flynn replied.

"You train more than any of the rest of us. It's one of the only things you do," Bi said. "Why don't you do something else?"

"There's nothing else for me to do," Flynn explained. "Zane and Ryan build things in their free time, Tarff cooks and eats food, you study, Blackeye does... whatever Blackeye does, but me? I specialize in combat. That's my talent."

"Well," Bi said. "I want you to find something else to do. I don't care what it is. It doesn't even have to be a new talent. Just do something peaceful. Something besides war." She walked partway down the stairs before turning back up to look at him. "Remember this, Flynn. To know your enemy is to gain victory, but to know yourself is far more important, as that allows you to gain freedom."

"Hey Bi," Flynn started, "I was wondering about the meeting-" He stopped as she disappeared down the stairs, either not hearing him or deciding not to answer. "Oh well I'll just ask her later." Flynn mumbled.

In most cases, Flynn would have been confused by the fact that Bi just randomly threw out a piece of wisdom he would not know what to do with, but he had gotten used to her doing that by now. He just wondered when it would be important.

Flynn entered his room and sat down on his bed. He tried to think of something to do. It was summer, so he had no homework. He didn't play any sports. He couldn't go hang out with any friends.

So, he became a normal kid. He picked up the remote, sat on his bed, and watched TV. What he saw actually surprised him.

"-Agent Jornavin says that the attack on the warehouse was not an unreasonable assault," A news girl said. "He has gotten news from an Enforcement officer saying that the Industry actually discovered the building was an IPA compound long before now, and they were preparing for the attack."

Flynn watched the screen intently. It was a news channel giving a report about a base that had been attacked in Arizona. Apparently the IPA soldiers had been forced to retreat during a skirmish with an Enforcement platoon and, after going back to their base, accidentally revealed their hideout's secret location.

Suddenly the handset phone in Flynn's room began to ring.

He didn't get very many calls from people outside the base. He normally called them. Curious, he picked it up. "Hello?"

"Flynn, did you hear about the Enforcement attack?" It was Emily.

"Oh," Flynn said. "Yeah."

"It's crazy what type of stuff they show on the news," she said. "One minute it will be about sports and then all of the sudden they switch to people being killed. How do they do it so casually?"

"I don't know," Flynn said. "It's crazy."

"Yeah," Emily responded. "And then people will move on as if nothing happened. It's almost like no one will even talk about it anymore."

"I remember those days when it was all over the news," Flynn said. "People evacuating from New York, raids happening all over the country. Now it's just what the news calls 'small things' like this in little pockets of the world. It's like everyone has stopped caring."

"I hate when the Industry does this," Emily said. She was upset again. Her being upset was just another reason that Flynn wanted to destroy Cadmore Industries until its name wasn't even remembered. "Why do they have to be so mean to these other people?"

"Don't know," Flynn said.

Emily sighed. "Well, I guess there is no use just complaining about it. What are you doing right now?"

"Nothing except talking to you," Flynn said. "Life is almost kind of boring."

"Well," Emily said. "Would you want to hang out tomorrow?"

Flynn smiled. "I'd love to."

Could Bi have known that Emily was going to call? Most people would call it impossible, but Bi was impossibly intelligent, and Flynn could think of nothing more peaceful, nothing further from war than being with Emily.

Flynn ended up talking to Emily for nearly five hours, until it got too late and they both went to bed. Neither of them really wanted to hang up, so they just laid there for a while. Flynn listened to the phone until he could hear Emily's heavy breathing on the other side. She had fallen asleep.

Flynn looked up at the ceiling. As much as he loved talking to her, it brought him so much pain. She was scheduled to die, and he had helped with that process. Then, possibly worst of all, was the fact that she believed that this organization was good.

Flynn slowly sat up as an idea began to form in his brain. He quickly threw on some shoes and his leather jacket and crept downstairs. He walked silently down the main floor hallway and into the garage. He then walked past the Rizen and into Zane's office.

Closing the door as quietly as he could, Flynn sat down in Zane's chair and turned on his computer, which had four monitors that took up most of one wall, along with an extra one on the desk. He decided to go with the one on the desk so his brain didn't hurt from all the different screens.

As the computer booted up, it asked for a passcode. Flynn tried to think.

Zane.

Nothing.

Ironborn.

Nothing.

Red Army.

Clan Vilo.

Rizen.

Flynn kept trying but to no avail. Eventually, a notification popped up on the screen that said he had one more chance until it would lock him out for twenty minutes. He leaned back in his chair and began thinking harder. Suddenly, the most random idea popped in his brain. He reached toward the computer but hesitated. Then he typed it in.

Blackeye.

The monitor flashed and pulled up the main screen.

"Well well well," he said to himself. "Seems like Zane's got a little secret he needs to tell the rest of us."

Flynn began to search the IPA files for any information on the extraction plan. He searched for nearly a half an hour and found nothing. He once again sat back in the chair and closed his eyes, half praying that he would be able to find something.

"Good evening Flynn." Flynn jumped and looked up. Zane was standing in the doorway with a glass of milk in his hands. "I must say it is a good night for web surfing."

Zane began to walk around to Flynn's side of the desk and he quickly closed out the files he had been searching.

Zane chuckled and pressed a button on his wrist screen, pulling the page back up. "If you're going to use my computer, I have a right to know why."

He leaned in front of the computer and began reading the things that Flynn had been searching for. "The Extraction Plan," he said, reading the search bar. "Well, I assume that you haven't found much, and I can tell you why."

"Why?" Flynn asked.

Zane pressed some more buttons on his wrist and swiped his finger across the small screen attached to it. "You've been searching in the wrong place." He leaned back against the wall and continued drinking his milk.

Flynn looked at the screen, where he had pulled up a file titled "The Extraction Plan." Flynn looked up at Zane in surprise. "How did you access this?"

Zane smiled. "Being one of the creators of a security system has its perks when you are trying to break into it."

Flynn looked back at the screen and scanned through the document. His eyes caught on some key phrases and he glanced through the rest, cycling through page after page of planned operation. "This is worse than I imagined."

"What is it?" Zane asked.

“For the sake of time,” Flynn said, “I can’t tell you. But, I will tell you this. Some of the leaders of the IPA are planning on using a project as a piece of bait for the Industry so they can find out where something is.”

Zane’s eyes widened. “Are you sure?”

“Yes,” Flynn said. “I overheard them talking about it in a meeting and now I have the proof right here. And they're doing it tonight. I have to go save her.”

Zane paused. “It’s a she,” he said, understanding coming to his eyes. “It’s Project 1711 isn’t it? That’s why they made you place the tracking beacon on her.”

“It doesn’t matter who it is,” Flynn said. “All projects are living people and that-”

Zane held up his hand. “Flynn, I know what you’re mean, but I also know how important she is to you. Based on the fact that you discovered my password, I believe you know what I mean.” He seemed to remember the past for a moment. “When I was saved by Sergeant Bi two years ago, she had one other soldier with her. This other soldier was literally the most beautiful and kind girl I had ever met. Bi told me that she was a member of Clan Pris, and would only be down here for a few weeks, so I gave her a necklace so she could remember me. After two years, I still haven’t forgotten her. It was only a few months ago that I was in the training room with Blackeye and she dropped something from one of her utility belt pouches. Even from all the way across the room, I could tell what it was. We made eye contact for a few seconds before continuing the training, and neither of us have spoken of it since. I haven't even seen the necklace after that." He paused as if remembering the experience before turning back to Flynn. He then pulled an object from his belt and tossed it to him.

Flynn caught it and looked at what it was. "The keys to the truck?" he asked in surprise.

"Well, I surely can't have you scratching up my Lamborghini," Zane smiled.

Flynn walked quickly across the office and opened the door before turning back to Zane. "Thank you."

Zane raised his nearly empty glass of milk and winked at him. "My pleasure."

18- The Extraction Plan

Hoover Avenue, Sacramento
California, U.S.A
10:30 p.m.
Flynn

Flynn sped down the road in the truck, hurrying as fast as he could. If the document was correct, then the extraction plan could have already started by now.

The IPA's plan was to "accidentally" leak information to get Enforcement to believe that Project 1711 was positive for Ironborn qualities and that they were moving her to safety tonight. The IPA believed the Industry would then intercept them and hoped a strategic retreat on their end would cause them to take their target instead of killing her. Then the IPA would take the opportunity to follow in pursuit. Flynn had to make sure neither of those things happened. Emily was now in even more danger, considering her parents were currently on vacation, which left it up to Flynn to save her.

Flynn was nearing Emily's house when two dots popped up on the truck's scanner. Enforcement helicopters. "Blast it," he cursed. Helicopters were always accompanied by a full platoon which, with two helicopters, was nearly fifty soldiers.

He began going faster down the suburban roads, twisting and turning at rapid speeds, when suddenly an Enforcement van blocked his path. He quickly swerved sideways and hopped out of the truck, engaging his suit and rolling on the asphalt as the soldiers recovered from their surprise and began firing at where Flynn hid behind the vehicle.

He grabbed his mataka, placed it on his head, and pulled his hiveblade off of his back. "Let's do this."

He stood and came out from behind the car, spinning his hiveblade to deflect each shot that approached him. Then, ducking down so his shield blocked his head, he charged the group of soldiers. When he was about to reach them, he jumped and spun through the air over the vehicle and onto the other side and began running away. As much as he would love to take out a squad of Enforcement troops, he needed to reach Emily.

Her small, red brick house was in sight now, flames licking up the sides of it and out the windows. "Fire," he mumbled to himself. "Why do the houses always have to be on fire?"

He ran towards it, pulling out his gun and shooting some soldiers that were standing farther away from the conflict who had not yet seen him. He saw a robot sniper on the roof of a house to his right and used his powers to lift it off the roof and pull it toward him. He heard a metallic crunch as it hit the ground behind him a few seconds later.

He reached the house's front porch just as he watched the IPA vehicles turning to leave, faking their retreat. He caught the glimpse of a soldier's eyes beneath his helmet as he hopped inside the Lander. They knew he was here.

Flynn continued battling the soldiers as the Landers sped away, feeling his hope fail when no one followed them. They were only here for the girl. And he was the only one protecting her.

He tried to make his way towards the front door as soldiers began to surround him, some shooting while others charged in. He battled fiercely, but knew he was overrun. He stepped backwards through the already-broken open door and into the burning house. Flames were everywhere around the front room that he had once sat in. He began running through the burning house, searching frantically for Emily. It didn't take long.

He ran into the living room and found her and her brother, Carter, trapped by flames and surrounded by Enforcement. Flynn swung his staff through them, breaking their circle. He took his mataka and flung it across the room at the bot nearest to Emily before pulling it back with his powers and using it to defend against the robots that now surrounded him. He quickly leveled the small group of bots and walked quickly toward Emily and her brother. He pulled the truck keys from his belt and tossed them to her. "Go save yourself. You need to get away from here as fast as you can."

As Emily looked into Flynn's eyes, the fear in them nearly shattered him into pieces. He had to stop himself from trying to comfort her. She couldn't know who he was.

Flynn was about to lead them out of the house when a shot from an Enforcement tank outside shattered the wall next to him into tiny splinters. He quickly grabbed Emily and Carter into him, protecting them from the blast. He felt a wave of force from behind him, Which sent him flying across the room and into a wall.

As he tried to get up, he realized that his helmet was broken over his left eye. He searched the room to find if Emily was alright and found her staring, horrified, at her brother, who had been hit by the blast and was now crumpled motionless on the floor. She ran to him and pulled his bloodied body into her arms. She then turned to Flynn, and the look she had in her eyes hurt him more than any explosion ever could. It was a look of sorrow. Of hatred. She held his eyes for a couple of seconds before the burning ceiling between them collapsed in, and Enforcement soldiers began charging into Flynn's section of the house.

Still motivated to keep Emily safe, he rose unsteadily and summoned his hiveblade and shield that had been dropped in the explosion. As the robots approached, he let out a cry and charged them head on, cutting down soldier after soldier, making it further and further through their ranks until he had exited the house.

For a brief moment he looked out over the multitude of soldiers. There were three vans and two helicopters with what looked like nearly eighty soldiers. He also caught a glimpse of his truck driving away down the road with no one in pursuit. Emily was safe now. It didn't matter if he died.

He checked his suit's status. Major damage in the helmet and running on fifty percent battery life. "Great," he mumbled to himself, and he ran into the fray. Emily might be mostly out of danger for now, but the Enforcement would keep looking for her if they didn't have another threat. All he needed to do was make a distraction.

As he fought the soldiers, he was instantly surrounded and, despite his best efforts, was too vulnerable to attacks, and his suit was losing its effectiveness. He continued cutting through, shooting, and bashing the robots, occasionally taking the time to throw one with his powers. He fought valiantly for about twenty seconds until an elite sniper from some distant location blasted him in the chest with a supercharge round, and he went flying out of the battle, along with pieces of Enforcement bots that came with him. The robots closed in on him as he struggled to get up, firing their guns rapidly. He felt like he was being pushed into the ground. He felt helpless.

Then, an idea came into his mind.

With all his strength, Flynn pushed himself to his feet and flung his mataka into the line of soldiers, dashing through the hole he had just made, making an all out sprint for one of the vans. When he arrived, he used his abilities to pull the driver through the door and onto the asphalt.

Flynn quickly hopped inside and slammed on the gas, swerving the van around and running over soldiers as they shot through the windshield. He could feel their attacks more now that his suit was slowly being ripped to shreds.

He had run a line through the bots and was turning around to make another run when one of the other vans rammed violently into his, shattering all the glass that remained and jerking Flynn to the side. He quickly recovered and swerved out of the way to make his run through the enemies, when to his dismay, the van followed him.

Flynn's vehicle was heavily damaged, so it was easily beat by the other van. The Enforcement driver pulled up next to him and began ramming Flynn's vehicle to the side while simultaneously shooting through the broken window.

Flynn looked up out of the hole that used to be his front windshield and saw that a third van was heading straight toward him. Acting quickly, he opened the door and dove out, hitting the ground roughly as his suit could no longer retain much of the impact. He looked up to see his van crash into the other one, causing a big explosion.

Flynn unsteadily tried to rise to his feet, but didn't have the strength. He was going to die here, on the battlefield, surrounded by his enemies. But Emily was safe now. He had succeeded.

Flynn looked up from where he was lying on the ground, wanting to look his enemies in the eyes. To his surprise, the soldiers were leaving. He heard an explosion and looked up to see one of the helicopters falling out of the sky, burning as it crashed to the ground. Behind where it had been was the Rizen, its machine guns blazing as it shredded through as many soldiers as it could without hurting any of the homes, even though they had already long since been abandoned.

Flynn watched in relief as the Rizen landed on the street and the last of the Enforcement robots scattered. He could see Zane and Tarff run down the off ramp and out into the road toward Flynn. Tarff scooped him up in his arms.

“Thank you,” Flynn mumbled.

“Don’t talk,” Tarff said. “You need your strength.”

“Actually, I have one question,” Zane said. “What have you done with my truck?”

That is when Flynn passed out.

19- Home Sweet Home

The Warehouse, Sacramento
California, U.S.A
9:00 a.m.
Talia

Soft light shone gently through the window as Flynn rested with Talia watching over him. After the Rizen had rescued Flynn, he had been asleep for nearly two days. During that time, Clan Captain Vilo and the rest of the board of officers had had a long debate about the subject of what would become of Scorpius. Now that they had decided, all they could do was wait for him to wake up.

Zane entered Flynn's room. "Still isn't up?" Talia shook her head. Zane sat down heavily in the chair across from her. His eyes were saddened, showing signs of confusion, and his back was slightly slumped over. Without him telling her, Talia had deduced that he had actually helped Flynn in his process in finding Emily and saving her. She herself wasn't exactly sure how to feel about the whole situation.

"Cago has gotten a lot of training today," Zane said, trying to start up a conversation.

Talia nodded. "He is getting a lot better."

Zane seemed to look off in the distance for a moment, as if thinking of what to say. "How did Flynn do it?" he finally asked.

"You mean fight so many enemies at once?" Talia asked. "Well, emotion is a strong force. I have felt a similar feeling that he did. It gets you to do things that you not only wouldn't do before, but couldn't do."

Zane nodded slowly. "So Emily-"

Suddenly, Flynn shifted and sat up, seemingly fully awake. He looked around the room with wide eyes for a second before realizing he was inside, and the threat was over. Whether or not he thought he was still fighting, or if he was dreaming about the firestorm again, Talia couldn't tell.

"Good morning Flynn." Bi did not seem at all surprised that he had suddenly woken up. Zane was still recovering from jumping back in surprise.

Flynn looked around him, studying the medical supplies and machines around his typically empty room. "What happened? Is Emily alright?"

"She's fine," Bi responded.

"Why is all of this stuff here?" he tried to get out of bed but stumbled and sat back down.

"Don't move too much, Flynn," Bi warned. "Even with Blackeye's healing, nineteen bullet wounds by itself is still severe, not to mention all of your other injuries."

"I'm fine," Flynn said gruffly. He slowly pushed himself up into a standing position.

Zane quickly ran and grabbed a black cane from the other side of the room. "Bi said you might need this. Your left leg was shattered in three places. I built it with some extra gadgets."

Flynn smiled lightly, taking the cane. "Thank you Zane." His voice was strained, and his expression was very tired. He looked down at his bandaged torso and leg and chuckled. "Guess I'll be out of action for a while."

"I'm afraid so Flynn," Bi said. "And for more than just your wounds."

Flynn turned towards her. "What do you mean?"

Bi sighed. "The board has decided that what you have done is a violation. You have been removed from the IPA."

"Removed?" he exclaimed.

"Yes," Bi said calmly. "They wanted you out of here as soon as you were fully conscious and standing up." She gestured towards him. "It seems like you have already done that."

Flynn ran a hand through his hair. “Well, I wouldn’t change my decision, even if I could.” He paused. “Where will I live?”

“Well, according to federal documents, you still own the apartment above the bakery,” Bi said. “I presume you could stay there.”

Flynn nodded. “School starts in four weeks. I guess I can just take the bus. It passes the bakery.” There was a pause. “Should I go get my stuff?”

“All of your things are already at the apartment,” Bi said. “I’ll drive you over as soon as you’re ready.”

Flynn sighed. “Well I guess there’s no point in waiting.” He leaned on his cane and began starting across the room. Bi stood and opened the door and they walked down the stairs into the garage.

“Where are the others?” Flynn asked.

Bi shrugged. “Most of them are just trying to keep going like normal. I was the only one that was supposed to have any contact with you. Zane just happened to be there when you woke up.”

Flynn nodded. Bi guessed that he probably wished that he could see the others one last time. They had been his family for nearly three years. “Proxy?” she said as they neared the Lamborghini.

“Yes?”

"Open garage door three."

"Affirmative." The door behind the Lamborghini opened as they got into the car and pulled away from the warehouse.

"There is one thing that I didn't tell you." Bi said as they drove. "I wanted to wait until Zane wasn't around."

"What is it?" Flynn wondered.

"Carter died during the extraction," Bi said.

"Emily's brother?" Flynn exclaimed. He had been hit by the explosion, but Flynn hadn't thought his injuries were that bad. At least he had tried to protect him.

"They are holding a funeral tomorrow," Bi continued. "I would think it appropriate for you to go."

Flynn nodded. Bi looked over and studied his eyes as he tried to hide what he was thinking. Fighting was almost his entire life. He had no family, no freedom, and almost no goals except for protecting what he already had. And now he was losing so much of it. At least he still had Emily. If he lost her...

They drove for about ten minutes, passing out of the dense forest near the warehouse and going into the city before they pulled up in front of the three-story bakery. It blended in with the rest of the older buildings that lined the road, each one looking similar to the next. The red brick bakery was on the bottom story with the apartment area in the two stories above it. It had a roof that doubled as a deck, and was decorated with white chairs and tables.

"Well," Bi said. "I guess this is goodbye for now." She turned toward him and shook his hand. "You're a good person, Flynn." Then, he felt a small object fall from her palm into his. He opened the door and exited the car. He used his cane to limp over to the sidewalk and watched as the car drove away.

He looked at the object in his hand. A pawn. Carved into a sphere topped cone with a circular pedestal at the bottom. He paused for a moment, staring at the small game piece as understanding came to him.

If Bi stood up for Flynn, it would be like the queen sacrificing herself for a pawn, leaving the rest of the pieces in helpless disarray, and most likely still causing the pawn to be removed from the game, even if it was slightly delayed. He looked back at where Bi had driven off. How had she known to teach him that lesson in the cockpit of the Rizen all those weeks ago? He shook his head. Bi seemed to know everything.

He turned and looked up at the building. "Home sweet home," he mumbled. Flynn reached to his belt. After all of the years, he had still kept the key. He walked up the steps and opened the door.

The inside was exactly how he remembered it. The dining area had dozens of tables and chairs, scattered neatly around the room. At the back was the curved pane of glass where customers could see the shelves that had once been full of baked goods. Behind that was the bakery itself, and behind that, in the far back right corner, were the stairs to the upper stories.

Flynn weaved slowly through the tables, remembering the smells that he would wake up to each morning as he would get ready for school, rush downstairs, and grab some already-made breakfast, straight from the bakery ovens.

Flynn's school had been an academy in the middle of the city, and he would bring some of his grandparents' treats there to let people try them. He had always loved that he could feel like he was helping his family earn more money.

Money was the reason his family had moved in with his grandparents in the first place. His dad had lost his job, and they could not continue with the house payment. Flynn's grandparents had always been so kind. His father, Jason, along with later his wife Maria, had been their only kids, and they were Flynn's only living grandparents. They had always spent so much time with his family, going on vacations, helping them with financial problems, and coming over for visits.

His grandfather, Montressor, was an archeologist. Although his heritage was mostly French, he loved studying asian culture, and would often visit there on his excursions. Occasionally, he would bring Flynn along, back before the money had gotten tight.

His grandmother, Martha, had been the one to start the bakery. His grandfather's parents had built it when they first moved here from Nebraska, but died before they could finish. Montressor eventually finished it himself and they had lived in it for nearly sixty years, making it the youngest building in this area of the city. That would change dramatically if he drove west, farther away from the warehouse, where skyscrapers were still being built.

Flynn's mom had actually been born in the upper story of the apartment. Grandfather had always told the story of how Maria had been so ready to get into the world, she just jumped right out! Later he would explain that that was not actually the case. His car had broken down, so they called a friend over but for some reason grandmother thought she wouldn't make it to the hospital. They called another friend, who was a nursemaid, and the baby was born in less than a few minutes.

His mother had always been one to get things done fast. When the money got bad, she had hopped in and gotten herself a part-time job as a substitute teacher before coming home and working at the bakery.

It was not that his father did not work hard. In fact, Flynn's father was one of the hardest workers Flynn had ever known. There just never seemed to be enough money even after his mom started helping. Flynn himself had not noticed the fact that they were in any trouble until on his ninth birthday his parents had said that he would not be able to go anywhere special and would have to do his party at home because they needed to save money. After that, more and more things began to be restricted, until a year later, they lost the house. Flynn had lived here for almost two years before-

He shut out his thoughts. He did not want to relive that memory any more than he already had to.

Flynn pushed through the waist-height spring-shutting door and walked behind the counter. He looked around for a moment before ascending the stairs. He saw that all of his things had been placed at the top in three suitcases. He rolled them down the hall to his room.

Opening the door brought back so many memories from the past. Spending time with his family, sneaking his friends in on a night when his family was gone, and eventually-

He pushed the thought out of his mind again.

He set the suitcases onto the ground and opened them. One was filled with clothes. The next had a few more clothes, along with all of his personal belongings. The last suitcase is what surprised Flynn. Wrapped neatly in a white cloth lay only three items. His mataka, his hiveblade, and his utility belt connected to his suit, which he guessed was now fixed. At the bottom was a piece of paper. *Stay safe*, it read.

Flynn sat back onto his knees. Who had put this here? It couldn't have been Cago, Zane, or Ryan because they knew that whoever was driving wouldn't be stupid enough to not check the luggage. Tarff, as nice as he was, would never do anything against protocol. Blackeye hadn't ever done anything to help anyone unless she was ordered to do it, which left it down to Bi. But why had she done it?

Flynn shook his head and sighed. A lot of confusing things have happened lately. Maybe now, without the war on his mind, he would be able to figure it all out.

20- A Grave Betrayal

St. Mary Cemetery, Sacramento
California, U.S.A
2:00 p.m.
Flynn

Flynn adjusted his tie as he walked down the concrete path. He had gotten a ride to the cemetery in a taxi and had shown up during the burial ceremony. The day was warm but the sun was covered by a blanket of clouds. The cemetery still bloomed with flowers that would soon die as the weather got colder.

Flynn exited the path and made his way over to the group of people gathered around the burial site, all wearing nice, black clothes. Flynn himself had on a black suit that Bi had gotten him nearly a year ago that he had almost never used. Occasionally, he had to lean on his cane when a pain shot up his left leg. He technically should not even be walking right now but he would not miss this for anything.

Flynn arrived, taking a position at the edge of the crowd. They were already done with all of the speeches and memories and now the crowd was giving condolences and revisiting with one another. When the casket came into view, so many bad memories flooded his mind that he had to force his eyes away from it. And the next thing he saw was even worse.

Sitting with her family, eyes red from tears, was Emily. He had managed to save her, but as glad as he was that she was alive, seeing her with any bit of sadness made Flynn want to do nothing more than comfort her. He felt so helpless knowing there was nothing that he could do. No enemy to kill. No battleship or juggernaut to destroy. Just an unbearable emotion.

Suddenly, Flynn realized that Emily was no longer seated in her seat with her family. He looked around for a second before he felt a tap on his shoulder. He turned and saw Emily standing beside him.

"You came," she said. She tried to smile but could not get herself to do it.

"Of course I came," he said. "Where else would I be?"

She sniffled and wiped her nose with the back of her sleeve. "Bi said that you got into an accident and you couldn't walk."

Flynn shook his head. "That wouldn't stop me from coming."

She leaned in closer and he put his arm around her. "Thank you Flynn," she whispered. She paused for a while and just looked at the grave. Flynn tried to read what she was thinking. He saw confusion in her eyes. She was uncertain about how to feel about something.

"They were there the night that he died, Flynn," she said. "The Ironborn."

Flynn blinked. "What do you mean?"

She took a staggered breath. "My parents had left me and Carter at the house so they could go on a vacation for their thirtieth wedding anniversary. They have left us many times, and we have not had any problems before. We were both about to get into bed when Carter saw three black vehicles pull up outside the front of our house. I recognized them from my research as IPA war vehicles called Landers. For a while the soldiers were out front, sitting in the Landers or occasionally stepping outside to converse with someone from one of the other vehicles. They all wore the easily recognizable IPA suits and helmets. Carter and I just sat watching them for a while, and they didn't do much. It wasn't until they all exited the Landers that we started getting worried.

"They began pulling out guns and other weapons, and getting into a defensive position as if preparing for an unseen enemy. Then that enemy showed up.

"Tons of Enforcement soldiers with their own version of the Landers, began speeding toward the IPA's defensive barrier, which was right in front of my house. The weird thing was, the IPA left as soon as they showed up. Apparently the Enforcement believed that the IPA was guarding me, so they stormed inside and surrounded me and my brother. As soon as they did, the IPA left." She looked confused as she told the story, as if still trying to figure out exactly what happened. "They weren't protecting me, Flynn. They were using me as bait so they could get away. It is exactly how they are shown on the news. They're evil."

Flynn swallowed, a mix of emotions coming to his mind. "None of them helped you?"

"There was one that did," she said. "But that was even worse than what the others did."

"What do you mean?" Flynn asked, confused.

"There was one soldier that was different from the others. He wore a shield-like helmet, and had a long double-bladed staff. He came into our burning house and destroyed the group of soldiers surrounding us. Then, he gave us the keys to a truck and told us to get away as fast as we could. For a moment, I thought my belief had not been wrong, that some of them could be good. But it was in vain. Just as he told us to leave, the front wall of the house shattered as it was hit by an explosive. The soldier quickly turned and pulled the nearest thing to him to shield himself from the explosion. That thing was my brother.

"The explosion threw the three of us across the room, and I landed near my brother. When I checked to see if he was alright, I nearly fainted. A foot-long piece of wood had embedded itself into his chest, and he was coughing up blood. I picked him up and looked over at the soldier who had done this. I will never forget the look he gave me. Fear. He feared for his life. He only feared for his own survival and would kill to keep himself alive."

Flynn felt like he had been the one impaled by a piece of wood. "But he tried to help you, didn't he?"

She shook her head. "The truck had been sabotaged. The tires were slashed and it ran out of gas in less than a mile. It would have been a perfect opportunity for Enforcement to follow me and the soldier to get away if he had not been so injured by the blast. With him immobilized, they didn't even seem to care about me."

"Are you sure it wasn't an accident?" Flynn asked. "What if he was trying to save you?"

She shook her head. "I considered that, Flynn. I really want to believe that they are good but..." She sniffled again. "There are just too many things that don't line up."

Flynn paused again. "What if-"

"Flynn," she cut him off. "Have you ever considered that the Industry might be right? That the IPA is evil? They killed my brother to keep themselves alive. There is just nothing else to it."

Flynn took in a deep breath. This was not what he had been expecting. He had tried to help! And now, just because the Enforcement had framed him by destroying the house and sabotaging the truck, they had turned her against what she believed. “So that’s it?”

Emily said nothing.

Flynn closed his eyes. All of this time, he thought that someone could finally see that the IPA was good. He had tried so hard to convince her that they were but yet, was it even true? Was she right? The IPA had set her up as bait. And, unknowingly, he had helped in that process. He kept telling himself that at least she was safe but to him that wasn’t enough. He had still failed.

“My mom wants me back over by the family,” Emily said, and Flynn opened his eyes. She stepped in forward and turned toward him. “I really want to believe they are good. I really do, Flynn. It is just that there is too much proof pointing against it. Not just what we see on the news but personal, firsthand proof.” She turned away. “At least try to consider it.”

As she walked back to her family, Flynn wondered what to do, and the answer came to him quickly. He would do what he had always done. He would fight for what he believed in. That, however, put another question in Flynn’s mind.

What did he believe in now?

INTERLUDE

21- Captain Dax

Enforcement Data Compound, Altadena
California, U.S.A
7:30 p.m.
Andrew

Clan Captain Dax walked confidently down the hall, long swords drawn, his metal boots thundering loudly each time they hit the ground. He wore his gleaming silver armor and blood red cape, storming forth like a titan from a legend. There was no need for stealth on this mission. There was never a need for stealth while Dax was around. He was invincible.

Andrew looked at his brother, who sat next to him. "Hey Gadget," he whispered. "How many rusties do you think we're gonna hit before Dax takes out the rest?"

Gadget chuckled. "Hardware, I would be surprised if we even see one of those puny things hide's with Dax around. Did you see the way Lieutenant Malikai acted around him? I've never seen him with any bit of respect for anyone but when Dax showed up," Gadget chuckled, "he looked like he was speaking to a god."

"Well, if my sources are accurate," Andrew said to his brother, "he's said to be the best soldier outside of the elite squad in Clan Troy."

In front of the two soldiers, Dax stopped. There were ten other soldiers with him, but it wasn't like he needed them. Everyone in Clan Dax was very strong and exceedingly large but the captain himself was a tank.

"I smell something," Dax said. "Gadget! Hardware! Scout ahead." He motioned one of his swords down the corridor. Andrew quickly pulled his gun out of its holster and ran in front of the rest of the group.

They were currently in a very large hallway in the heart of an Enforcement base. They had sent in a squad from Clan Vilo to get a piece of information stored on a computer here. The squad had gotten to the base, but the forces inside were too powerful for them to handle on their own.

So they sent Dax.

The two soldiers reached a door. Andrew turned toward Gadget, who had already pulled out his tools to disengage the lock. He didn't have his nickname for nothing.

They were through the door in seconds and they entered the room. It was extremely large, and looked like some kind of factory, but it was too dark to see anything. Andrew turned on the flashlight on his gun. The two soldiers began walking through the room, scanning the area for any enemies. Behind them, Dax and the other soldiers entered the room and fanned out.

"Hey Hardware," Gadget said. "Come check this out."

Andrew walked over to him. "What is it?"

"Some kind of piece of machinery. This might give us an idea of what they are building. Do you recognize it?" he asked.

Andrew bent down and studied the piece of metal. "This goes to a robot alright. I think I might recognize its design. It almost looks like the arm of a..." He trailed off.

"What?" Gadget said.

A pile of scrap metal exploded, sending shrapnel across the room. From underneath it rose a massive robot that nearly reached the ceiling, its twin cannons blazing.

"A juggernaut," Andrew breathed.

Near the juggernaut, Dax raised his sword and gave a growling war cry.

Gadget raised his gun toward the robot. "You are so screwed."

Dax charged the juggernaut, ramming his shoulder into it. Dax was huge, but he barely measured up to the middle of the robot.

The bot regained its balance and faced its attacker as they began wrestling each other. All around the room, Enforcement robots began rising up from piles of scrap metal like creatures emerging from a swamp, filling the air with gunfire.

Gadget and Andrew stood back to back, firing on the soldiers around them as Dax fought with the juggernaut.

"Well, you were wrong, Gadget," Andrew said over the noise. "Dax is here, but I can still see these robots."

Gadget pulled a grenade from his belt and threw it across the room, destroying a cluster of enemies. "Well I didn't expect a juggernaut to show up," he justified.

As the robots grew nearer, Andrew picked one up and threw it at another one. He then turned and punched one in the face. "There are too many of them," he said to Gadget. "Double time?"

Gadget smiled. "Is there any other way?"

Andrew leaned back against Gadget, but instead of colliding into him, he melted into his body like they were both made out of liquid, forming a giant-sized hybrid version of the two soldiers.

The super soldier leveled its two guns at its enemies, which now seemed much smaller than before.

A loud crashing sound came from the other side of the room and a cheer went up from the soldiers. The juggernaut was down. The rest of the robots began to disperse and with the help of Dax, they were eliminated quickly. Gadget and Andrew separated and walked over to where the rest of the soldiers were gathered around Dax.

"The data file we need is somewhere inside of this base," he was saying. "We need to split up to find it. But be alert. There may be more enemies still alive."

The group split up, taking different exits out of the main room. Andrew followed Gadget to the right, where he led them out a door and up some stairs. The base itself was multiple stories tall, made solidly of metal, the only lighting being a few fluorescent strips placed periodically on the ceiling.

Gadget led Andrew to a door, reaching forward and opening it slowly. It was a dark computer storage room with rack after rack of computer towers. The chip could be in any one of them. Two Enforcement guards were stationed inside, but they were taken out before they could even raise their guns.

"Find a tower with the mark 34-D1," Gadget told him.

The two of them split up. Andrew started down one of the rows of towers, studying each number. He reached up and turned on his thermal scanner on his helmet. "Hey Gadget, are you seeing this?" he asked.

"Seeing what?"

"Turn on your thermal scanner."

Andrew heard a click from the other side of the room. "This doesn't make sense," Gadget said. "According to the scanner, there are robots everywhere."

Andrew heard a scuttling noise at the base of his foot. He pulled out his gun and shot at where the noise came from.

A wisp of smoke came up from a tiny little robot that was designed like a spider, with tiny little eyes on its head. "That's because they are."

Tons of tiny spider droids began pouring from the shelves of computer towers. Andrew began shooting at every bot he could see, but he couldn't fire fast enough, and they began to overwhelm him.

"Run, Hardware!" he heard Gadget say.

Andrew turned and tried to get out of the small hallway he was in. The shelves were so close together that he had to move sideways. The bugs, due to their small size, were faster.

Looking up, he could see that Gadget was in a similar predicament. He watched as his brother got swarmed by the tiny robots and disappeared.

The bugs began flooding in from all sides of the room, coming through the ventilation grate, from a small hole in the corner in the wall, everywhere.

Andrew threw a grenade to destroy some of the robots but it was no use. He struggled as they rushed over him, covering his entire body in a blanket of metal and attacking his suit. There was nothing he could do. He watched as his suit's battery life began to drain. Eighty percent. Seventy percent. Fifty percent. Andrew could feel his own life draining away. Once his suit was gone, the robots would tear into his skin, and he would be ripped to shreds.

Andrew heard a loud bang and then the sound of bullets firing across the room. The layer of robots began to disperse. He looked up and saw Dax standing in the doorway, dual fully-automatic guns blazing. His armor sparked with electricity, killing all of the bugs as they tried to swarm him. All the spiders were gone in a matter of seconds.

Maybe Lieutenant Malikai had been right. Maybe he was a god.

"Come." He beckoned Gadget and Andrew through the doorway. "One of the other groups found the data chip. Now that the air cannons are down, we have called in an air strike on the rest of the factory. It's time to leave."

PART III

SAVING A DREAM

22- Rooftops

The Bakery, Sacramento
California, U.S.A
8:30 p.m.
Flynn

Flynn flipped through another page in his grandfather's journal. He enjoyed reading about everything that young Montressor had done when he was Flynn's age.

At that time, they had called him Monte. He had always been interested in artifacts from the past, and studying them later became his profession. He always said that despite all his years of searching for precious items, he found the most valuable thing of all in his home town of Sacramento. Flynn's grandmother. To Montressor, he couldn't have ever found anything better.

It had been a month since Carter's funeral, and most of Flynn's days consisted of reading and watching the news, and most of his nights were spent talking to Emily on the phone.

The only other thing keeping his life interesting was his squad. Vilo had told Bi that if Flynn apologized for what he had done, and promised not to break the rules again, then they would welcome him back. His squad had called to let him know this, and now called nearly every day, trying to use a new approach each time to convince him to come back. The squad would be much better with him, that he could believe. He believed he could apologize as well, but he couldn't get himself to promise that he wouldn't try to save her if they tried again.

As he sat, thinking about what to do, the phone rang. "Here we go again," he said as he picked it up. "Hello?"

"Flynn." Cago. It was usually Cago. "Look, Flynn, we're not going to try to convince you to come back anymore. But we have one last thing for you."

"What is it?" Flynn asked.

"Go to the roof," Cago said.

"Why?" he asked.

"You'll see when you get there." He hung up.

Flynn set the phone down and debated on what he should do. After deciding that nothing bad could come from it, he started walking up the stairs. After the first flight, he passed his room. He paused for a moment. Should he take his mataka with him? Or his hiveblade? He decided against it and continued walking.

Flynn went up the second flight of stairs. Since arriving at the house, he hadn't gone to the third floor. As he arrived at the top, he saw that the door to his grandfather's office was open.

Memories flooded into him. His parents carrying him up the stairs and to the roof, where both of them died. Then ten year old Flynn becoming surrounded by the enemy robots before jumping off the edge of the roof, grabbing onto the railing, and swinging into his grandfather's office. The office looked the same. The doorway was splintered from Enforcement trying to get inside, the cabinet was still broken where Flynn had grabbed out the only two weapons his grandfather had had in his office. The two weapons that he had found in China.

The hiveblade and mataka had saved him that night. Without them, he would have never lived long enough for the IPA to come save him. He remembered Bi's hand reaching through the broken window, lifting him out and onto the gangway of a ship, the ship they had had before they got the Rizen.

All of these memories came and passed in an instant. Flynn found himself nearly in tears. This was why he didn't come to the third story of the bakery.

He pressed on, striding toward the final staircase, the one that led to the roof. When he got to the top, he hesitated. Then he turned the handle and pushed open the door.

The roof was just how he remembered it. The chairs lining his left side, the now-abandoned roof garden on his right, everything was the same. He could even see the exact spot where he had used the small lip on the edge of the roof to climb into his grandfather's office that night all those years ago.

He closed the door and turned to the back side of the building, where the sun was setting in the distance. And there, standing perfectly, like someone from a movie, her brown hair falling gracefully past her shoulders, her dark blue eyes matching her perfect smile, was Emily.

"Emily?" Flynn asked, stunned. "What are you doing up here?"

She walked toward him, still smiling. "Cago sent me."

Flynn sighed. "Of course he did."

Emily's smile faded slightly. "What is wrong with Cago?"

"Nothing," Flynn said quickly. "Did he tell you to try to convince me to do something?"

She looked confused. "No. He wanted me to give you this." She pulled a letter out of her back pocket and handed it to him.

He opened it and read it.

Flynn,

We have gotten some news from Zane. He was doing some of his nerdy research stuff when he found more information about the extraction plan. They are going to try it again. Only this time, the Industry is going to use the Blood Squad. They are coming into Periman dock on a boat called the Santa Maria. Flynn, we all would want to try to stop you from hopelessly protecting her, but if we cannot, we at least wanted to give you a hero's send off.

-Cago

Understanding flooded into Flynn's mind. His squad was not trying to use Emily to convince him to stop protecting her. They were trying to give him a chance to say goodbye to her.

Before he died.

He looked up into Emily's eyes. They were so bright, so beautiful, so full of hope. She had no idea what was about to happen. She had no idea that the five most skilled assassins in the world were coming after her. She had no idea what he had done. And for a moment, all he wanted to do was stand there and be with her. To never have to look away from those eyes.

But he needed to protect her. The Blood Squad was coming and he was the only thing stopping them.

She must have seen his expression because her smile faded completely. "What's wrong?"

Flynn took a deep breath. She hated the Ironborn now. If he told her that he was one of them... "I don't have time to explain."

"Can I help?"

He rubbed his forehead, trying to figure out exactly what he was going to do. "Look, if you want to know what's going on, go talk to Cago, and have him speak with Bi. She will know what to do. Tell them to tell you everything. Then, if you want to help, meet me at Periman dock." He paused. Then he added, "if you're still sure you don't hate me."

She gave him a concerned look. "Flynn, why on earth would I hate-"

That is when he kissed her.

It was a soft, lingering kiss, but Flynn knew he would remember it for the rest of his life.

Which might not be a very long time.

He pulled away and walked backward toward the edge of the roof until he felt his foot hit the small lip that was now the only thing that was in between him and three stories of freefall. Emily stood still, too stunned to move. For the first time in a while, Flynn smiled.

"I love you."

With a salute, he leaned backward and fell off the building.

23- Truth

The Bakery, Sacramento
California, U.S.A
9:00 p.m.
Emily

Watching Flynn fall off of a three-story building finally woke Emily up from the shock that he had just kissed her.

She ran to the edge in horror but when she looked down to the street below, he was nowhere to be seen.

Emily shook her head. She needed to figure out what was going on. She had never seen Flynn so concerned before. If he was in trouble, she needed to help.

Emily walked to the back of the roof and, locating the built-in ladder that she had used to get up, climbed down to the ground. She was now in the alleyway behind the building. Pulling out her phone, she dialed Cago's number, which she had gotten at the party a few weeks ago.

"Cago?" she asked as soon as she heard him pick up.

"How did it go?" he asked.

“I’m not sure,” she replied. “He told me to talk to you. He said Bi could explain but I don’t even know who that-”

“Where are you now?” Cago asked.

“Outside the bakery,” she replied.

Cago sighed. “He told you he wanted you to know everything?”

“Yes but I don’t know-”

“Just wait there,” Cago said. “I’ll come get you.” He hung up.

Emily pocketed her phone, walking out to the front side of the bakery, pacing back and forth in worry. The ten minutes it took before a car finally pulled down the road seemed like an eternity.

The Lamborghini stopped in front of her, and the passenger window rolled down.

“Get in,” she heard.

As she got into the front seat, she was surprised at the interior’s design with its high-tech dashboard, lights, and doors that were nearly twice as thick as a normal car.

She was surprised when she saw Cago was in the driver's seat.

"What?" he said, igniting the engine and pulling down the road. "This situation is much more important than me not having my license yet." She watched curiously as he pulled a box-shaped microphone from the dashboard. "This is Shadow to base, we have a code 55 on Project 1711, over."

"Shadow, please repeat the last message." Emily heard an undistinguishable voice come through the other end.

"I repeat, code 55 on 1711."

"Are you sure?" the voice asked.

"Yep," Cago responded as they began to drive east. "Orders from Scorpius."

"Copy that," the voice said. "You are clear for code 55 initiation."

Cago put the microphone back. He sighed and turned toward her. "Emily, there are things that Flynn hasn't told you."

Oh no, Emily thought. *This cannot be good.*

"Apparently, he trusts you enough to have us tell you everything but I must warn you. This is dangerous information."

She nodded. "If it will help him, I want to know."

Cago took a deep breath. "Emily, Flynn has been part of an undercover army working against Cadmore Industries for the past three and a half years."

Emily was almost as shocked as when Flynn had fallen off of the roof. Almost. "You mean the IPA?"

"Yes," Cago responded. "And so am I. We are in Clan Vilo, in Den Exon, under the direction of Squad Sergeant Bi, who is one of the smartest intellectuals on the planet. We are both Ironborn, and we both have powers that definitely help us in war, but fighting is not our speciality. Instead, we find projects. Projects are people in our area that the IPA believes may have powers. You, for example, are Project 1711. Flynn was assigned to study you."

Emily froze as a thought came to her mind. "So Flynn was only interested in me because he thought I had powers?"

Cago laughed. "Yeah, right. Flynn has been interested in you for a lot longer than the IPA has ever existed."

Emily blushed. "Oh. I have only known him for a year."

"Well, he has known of you for a lot longer than that," Cago said. "But that is off-topic. According to Flynn's observations, you supported the IPA, and the Ironborn as a whole in the past, but now, due to the situation with your brother, you have turned against that idea."

Emily paused for a moment, watching out the window for a moment as they passed out of the city and began driving through a thick forest. "Well, not exactly. It's just, I believed for so long without any proof that they were good but when I finally saw them firsthand, they weren't good at all. Maybe that isn't the whole IPA, though. Maybe it was just that group of people at my house, along with the one that killed Carter."

Cago's face fell.

"What?" Emily asked.

Cago struggled to find his next sentence. "Emily, what if I told you that the soldier who was there that night, the one that killed Carter, was Flynn?"

Emily's eyes grew wide. "No. He wouldn't do that. He wouldn't just kill someone innocent."

"Of course he wouldn't," Cago said. "Allow me to explain. First of all, just because we are in the IPA does not mean we agree with everyone else in it. Now, normally, if a soldier in the IPA gets caught by Enforcement then they get killed. However, recently, they have been disappearing. Getting taken instead of killed. To solve this situation, some of the high-ranking officers in Clan Vilo set up an operation called the Extraction Plan. Their idea with the Extraction Plan was to use a project as bait, because using a soldier would be too wasteful. They purposefully leaked information about you having powers to Cadmore Industries to get them to try to capture you. They also had

Flynn place a tracking device on you, telling him it was for your safety, when really it was because they wanted to be able to know where you went after you were captured. Well, as you can imagine, when Flynn accidentally found out about this he was furious but also conflicted. So, on the night that you were scheduled to be taken by Enforcement, he went to save you. When he showed up, the IPA was leaving, and he was hopelessly outnumbered, but that didn't stop him. He got to your house, killing every Enforcement robot in the way, and then gave you the keys to Zane's truck so you could get away. When the wall exploded, he tried to protect you and Carter from the blast. He had no idea that it would later kill him, or that the truck had been sabotaged by the Enforcement."

Emily took a deep breath, taking it all in. "So that's why he was saying I would hate him." She paused for a long time. "I had no idea that was what he was trying to do. I would have never..." She suddenly realized something. "At the funeral, when I told him my side of the story, that must have destroyed him!"

"It did more than that," Cago said. "He got kicked out of the IPA for what he did, and it turned out to all be for nothing, because now you hated him anyway."

"No! I didn't mean..." she stopped. What had she meant? Did her perspective change just because it had been Flynn? *No. Not because of Flynn,* she thought, *but because of his intentions.*

"I guess the real question is, were we right?" Cago asked. "About you having powers, I mean."

She shook her head. "I never lied to Flynn. I'm just a normal girl that thinks all humans should be equal."

"That's what we believe too," Cago replied. "Sadly most people disagree, which allows Enforcement to kill us all off."

Emily paused. "That night, at the party, you guys didn't leave because Flynn's parents needed him home, did you?"

Cago nodded, confirming her theory. "Both of us nearly died that night."

"How are his parents letting him risk his life like this?" Emily asked.

Cago hesitated, an odd look coming to his eyes.

"What?" Emily asked.

"Did you ever meet Flynn's parents?"

"Flynn has shown me videos of them together," Emily remarked.

"In person."

She thought for a moment, understanding coming to her. "No..."

Cago's face told her all she needed to know. "Three years ago," he said. "Enforcement was trying to get to Flynn, just like they were trying to get to you."

"But the videos," Emily said.

"We have the best technology in the world and you don't think we could fake a few videos?" Cago asked.

"I get that," she said, "But why? Why wouldn't he just tell me?"

"To keep you safe," Cago said. "That's why he's done all of this. Flynn put so much of his life into protecting you and now he fears it is all going to waste. Clearly, based on where he is now going, he still has faith."

"Where is he going?" Emily asked as the Lamborghini pulled up out of the forest and a large warehouse came into view. Emily saw five people standing in front of it. Two were clearly twins, one was a large Polynesian, another was a young lady with dark skin and a messy afro who was clearly the oldest of the group, and the last was a soldier in full armor. She was taller than the twins and obviously female.

"Who are they?" Emily asked.

"Our squad," Cago said. "I imagine you will be acquainted shortly. But you asked me where Flynn was going. The best answer I can give you right now," he let out a deep breath, "Is to his death, Emily. He is going to his death."

24- Blood Squad

Periman Dock, Bodega Bay
California, U.S.A
11:00 p.m.
Flynn

Flynn sprinted down the road as hard as he could. He had been running for a while now, nearly forty miles, but with the help of his suit, he had done it in under two hours.

After leaving Emily, he had done the same trick that he had used the night his parents had died, grabbing the railing and swinging through the window into the office. He would have to fix it when he got back. Or maybe the new owners would fix it when he didn't.

He had then grabbed his hiveblade, mataka, and suit from his suitcase, and exited the building. Now, nearly two hours later, he was at the dock.

Periman Dock was at the end of a long road, an outcropping of metal sticking out from the rocky cliffs at the edge of the ocean. Flynn stood outside of the fence, looking at a *Restricted Area* sign. He could just use his powers to jump over the fence, but he wanted to save as much energy as possible.

Reaching forward, he gripped the area around the sign and began climbing. It was not like the authorities were going to hurt him while the Blood Squad was there.

After climbing down the other side of the fence, Flynn ducked down, trying to stay hidden. The interior of the dock was full of large stacks of shipping containers. This dock was normally used for taking in shipments from cargo boats.

Flynn crept along the edge of the containers and studied the way they were placed. They made a maze-like design of walls, most of the stacks being two or three crates high, about ten feet a crate. With his powers, Flynn could use this to his advantage.

He moved slowly and carefully down the row of containers, turning around corners multiple times before getting to the middle of the loading bay where there was a huge yellow crane, unloading crates from a cargo boat that was about forty feet below the dock in the water.

On the side of the boat read the words *Santa Maria* and on the deck, in plain sight, were five of the most fearsome robots Flynn had ever seen.

Flynn quickly tried to remember all that he could about the Blood Squad. First, they were the most powerful and high tech robots that David Cadmore had ever built, but he had only gotten five finished before he died, and Caleb could not replicate them. It was rumored that there were two more that stood as his personal guards, but it had never been confirmed.

He also knew that they were built like a normal C.I. squad. The tallest of the five had been nicknamed Bull, and for good reason. He was larger than a juggernaut, and stronger too. He was the strength specialist.

The leader's name was Shark. Sharks love blood, hence the name of the squad.

Their sniper was named Falcon. He had extremely powerful sensors, and could see on all sides.

The stealth specialist was Fox. His exoskeleton could turn invisible while he was fighting, except for when he got hit.

Last was the gunner. Wolf. Wolf was probably the most famous of the Blood Squad because he was said to have dueled Clan Captain Troy in a fight and Troy had barely survived.

Flynn watched as the crane kept picking up crates from the boat. He waited there for nearly half an hour before Shark gave a signal to the rest of his squad. They all used jetpacks to fly up to the dock, except for Bull, who just climbed up the forty-foot cliff face to the dock with his hands. The cargo boat rocked and made huge waves as he stepped off.

Flynn took a deep breath in as he turned the safety off of his gun. This was it. He probably only had minutes to live. Every second counted now. He was going to save Emily, or die trying.

He silently aimed his gun toward the group, who was walking across the dock. He decided to aim his first shot at Fox, while he was still visible. He waited until they passed the crane. Then, he pulled the trigger.

The whole squad turned toward Fox as Flynn dove out of the way and then passed out of sight. He began running through the crates, diving from the middle in a different way than he had come. After a moment, he paused and turned on his thermal scanner. The squad was splitting up. Perfect.

Wolf was walking north, Shark east, and Bull south toward Flynn. Falcon had somehow already gotten on top of the crane and was now looking through his scope to find Flynn. Fox was nowhere to be found, even on Flynn's thermal scanners.

Apparently David, like Clan Xion, had figured out how to cloak heat rays. That could be a problem.

Flynn began creeping along the side of the containers, setting explosives along his way. He made it about forty feet before he got slammed into by an unseen force and knocked to the ground.

"Oh, this is like Cago all over again," Flynn mumbled. On the thermal scanner, the rest of the squad had changed course and was now headed his way.

He pulled out his shield and threw it in the direction that the attack had come from but hit nothing.

Something grabbed his throat and Fox suddenly became visible behind him, putting him in a chokehold. Thinking quickly, Flynn used his powers to summon his shield to his head, but ducked at the last second, causing the mataka to hit Fox directly in the face and sending him sprawling to the ground.

Flynn pulled his shield from the ground to the holster on his arm and leapt toward Fox. Using the momentum of his jump, along with his powers, Flynn stabbed the robot straight through the neck with his staff, and the tip of his blade cut a few inches into the concrete ground. Fox sputtered for a moment before dying.

Flynn stood up. "Well that wasn't too hard."

Another force slammed into his back with the power of a moving semi truck. As Flynn struggled to rise to his feet, he thought he had been hit by Bull, but when he turned around, he discovered that it had only been Wolf's handgun. Instead of the bullet going through him, his suit had absorbed the energy and dispersed it across his entire body. Apparently that meant if the bullet was strong enough, it could send him flying five feet through the air.

"Well that's just great," Flynn said. He lunged to the side to avoid another bullet and leapt on top of the crates, using his powers to propel him upward.

Flynn had never been afraid of heights. Instead, being thirty feet up reminded him of his recent experience on the bakery's rooftop. It reminded him of Emily. The memory gave him strength.

Flynn quickly calculated the movements of each soldier. Shark was moving on the left side of the crates, and Bull on his right, both of them coming toward him. Wolf was behind him now, using his jetpack to fly up to the top of the containers.

Flynn began running toward Bull and Shark, shooting at Wolf over his shoulder. Any bullets that actually hit the robot did not seem to affect him much.

As Flynn neared the two approaching soldiers, he readied his shield and took a deep breath. Then, making sure not to lose his footing, he lunged to his left, doing a side-flip over the gap between the two stacks of crates while throwing his shield at Shark.

Flynn watched Shark get knocked to the ground as he landed. He summoned his makata and kept running. His only chance was to separate them and take them out one by one.

Out of the corner of his eye, Flynn saw a tiny movement and turned. Falcon was about to fire.

Quickly, Flynn threw his mataka at the sniper, but it was too late. Flynn watched the robot get knocked from the crane just as he got thrown to the side by one of Falcon's bullets, falling off of the crate and landing roughly on the ground.

Grunting, he stood up. He heard pounding footsteps from his left and turned just in time to see Bull smash through the stack of crates, sending them flying through the air. Wolf and Shark followed behind him, and they started firing their guns, once again knocking Flynn to the ground.

"Stop," Shark said. Wolf hesitated. "This one is strong. The boss will want him alive."

Flynn reached down to his wrist and pressed a button, setting off the explosives. The wall of crates behind the robots began to fall on top of them.

Wolf and Shark dove out of the way, but Bull just let the crates bounce off of him, doing little damage.

Flynn leapt into the air, using the distraction to help him get farther away. He did a backflip over the wall of crates behind him and kept moving, his hiveblade ready. He turned around a corner and was surprised to run straight into Falcon, impaling him with the tip of his staff. The robot crumpled to the ground.

"Sorry about that."

Flynn continued running until he again reached the middle of the dock. As soon as he stepped out in the open, he felt a weight hit him in the chest, sending him flying toward the end of the dock. He looked over the edge behind him as wave after wave crashed into the rocky cliff.

He stood up and saw Wolf sprinting toward him, knife in hand. Flynn waited in a crouched position, gun held ready. Right as Wolf was about to reach him and plunge the knife into his chest, Flynn pulled out his staff and ducked down, stabbing the robot's abdomen.

The momentum sent Wolf sprawling over the edge with the hiveblade in his chest, and he fell off of the cliff into the water.

Flynn watched as the other two robots ran into the clearing. Bull was carrying one of the crates, and he threw it at Flynn.

He quickly rolled out of the way, hiding behind a wall of crates. It was not until now that Flynn realized how tired he was. His suit was running on ten percent power and was nearly ripped to shreds and he was bleeding in many places. He had not even noticed the small knife that Falcon had embedded into his chest before he died. He pulled it out. He did not care about his wounds. Every shot he took was another one that would not be going to Emily. That was his only drive now. That was all he cared about.

Readying his gun, Flynn ran around the corner and sprinted toward Shark, knife raised. He fired his gun harmlessly multiple times until Shark pulled out his blaster and shot Flynn in the chest. This time he did not get thrown back. His suit was dead. The bullet went straight through him. He staggered for a moment before pushing through the pain. He continued running.

Flynn raised his mataka as he neared his enemy and brought it down with all the force he could muster. Before it reached its target however, Shark punched him in the side of the head, and he went sprawling to the ground, the mataka falling out of his grasp as it slid across the deck. Reaching up to his face, Flynn could feel his jawbone as it had broken and split through his skin.

"How sad," Shark said as he walked up to Flynn. Flynn could barely hear him as he tried to push through the pain. "You would have been a great test subject for the Rift. Now you will have to die." Flynn could now see that a symbol was painted on the side of the robot's forehead. It was a white fist, clasped around a narrow blade. For a moment, he wondered what it was for, before his attention switched to the gun pointing at his chest.

"I must save her," Flynn mumbled, trying to regain strength.

"What was that?" Shark asked.

Flynn jumped up and kicked the gun out of Shark's hand, sending it clattering across the floor. He then plunged the knife into Shark's neck.

It did nothing.

Shark pulled the knife out and stabbed it into Flynn. Flynn tried to summon his shield but Bull hit it out of the air, sending it flying away.

Shark pulled out a second gun and pulled the trigger. Flynn felt nothing. He couldn't. All feelings were gone. Shark pulled the trigger again. And again.

"I can't die," Flynn said to himself, barely whispering this time. "I have to," he started coughing up blood, "save her." Flynn tried to stand up again but took a bullet to the knee and collapsed.

Then, he heard a noise behind him. Turning, Flynn saw Wolf, walking toward him with the hiveblade protruding from his chest. Behind him were Fox and Falcon.

"Well well well," Wolf said. "Look who finally gave up."

"Non-biological regeneration," Flynn gasped. "Impossible." He started coughing again.

"Maybe to your friends back at Xion," Wolf said. He pulled out the staff. The hole in his chest closed itself, leaving no mark. "Here is your weapon." He tossed the hiveblade on the ground next to Flynn. He then pulled out his gun and pointed it at Flynn's chest.

This is it, Flynn thought. *The end of everything. At least I got to say goodbye to Emily. At least I got to protect her.*

At that moment, Flynn again saw movement out of the corner of his eye. He turned toward the movement, and what he saw surprised him. Standing on top of the stack of crates, in full armor, was Bi and the rest of the squad. Then he noticed one more. He didn't even have to see her face to know who it was.

Emily.

"Don't worry Flynn, we're here," He heard Emily's voice say through his helmet. Apparently his comm was still working.

Wolf looked up and saw the seven soldiers on top of the wall. Seeing that he had noticed, they all ducked down. All of them except Emily.

Wolf pulled the trigger. Flynn watched as Emily staggered for a moment and then fell forward off of the crate. She didn't have a suit on.

"No!" Flynn grabbed his hiveblade and stood up, lunging at Wolf.

Wolf shot at Flynn, but he ignored the attack, and cut the robot in half.

Falcon and Fox both fired their guns at Flynn but he ran toward them anyways. For a second, they seemed unsure what to do, as if they were confused at why he still hadn't died. That uncertainty was gone in seconds however, as Flynn reached them and they met their own demise.

As Flynn turned around, he had about half a second to see that Wolf was already beginning to heal before he got rammed into by Bull, lifted twenty feet into the air, and then body slammed into the ground.

With the crushing weight on top of him, Flynn could no longer breathe. He had failed. Emily was dead, and he had failed.

Cago looked up into the sky and watched as the Rizen fired its massive guns into the biggest of the robots. The robot staggered for a moment before collapsing to the ground.

He then watched as a small ship took off from the cargo boat next to the loading bay. The leader had gotten away.

Tarff and Bi began separating the parts of the other robots that had fallen. It had not taken them long to discover that they could heal themselves if their parts stayed too close together. Bi then spoke some words to Tarff, and he began carrying the pieces to the Rizen, which was now landing near the crane.

Seeing that the threats were gone, Cago ran over to Flynn. Blackeye was already there, trying to heal him. It was not doing very much. Flynn was bleeding a ton, and

Cago could see parts of multiple of his bones. He was mumbling something incoherently.

"Stay with us Flynn," Cago said. "We won. It's over. We can go home now." Flynn did not seem to hear. His eyes were glazed over. "Come on Flynn, we need you. Emily needs you."

A small bit of life seemed to come back into his eyes. "Emily?" he mumbled.

"Yes."

He began coughing. "Emily is dead."

"No," Cago said. "That was just a decoy, Flynn. A robot marked with her DNA. She's alive."

"Got to get back-" Flynn continued, "for the Redstone."

"The Redstone?" Cago asked. "Isn't that the project that Clan Troy is doing?"

"Yes," Bi said as she approached from behind Cago. "But its name originated from a constellation. The Redstone is the thing that is most important to you in your life. Something you are willing to die for. My guess is he speaks of Emily."

"I must stay for the Redstone," Flynn said again.

"Yes," Cago said. "Stay alive for the Redstone."

"But the Redstone is dead," Flynn's eyes continued to glaze over. "I go to her."

"No!" Cago grabbed Flynn's shoulders. "You have to stay! She's alive!"

"He can't hear you," Blackeye said. Cago turned toward her in surprise. She had never spoken before. Through her voice scrambler, her voice sounded deep and almost electronic, like a robot. "His brain is no longer receiving information. By the time he comprehends what you are saying, he will be dead."

"No," Cago whispered this time. He turned to look toward the Rizen, where Emily was running over to where Flynn was laying on the ground. She held Cago's knife in her hand. That knife had saved his life multiple times but right now her life was the one that needed to be safe.

She knelt next to Flynn as Cago put his arm around her shoulder. "He is gone," he said softly.

Emily began crying and buried her face in her hands. Cago looked down at the ground. This is not what Flynn would have wanted. He had paid with his life for Emily to be happy.

She sniffled and grabbed Flynn's hand. "I just wish I would have known what he was going through. I wish he would have told me."

Flynn opened his eyes slightly. "Emily?" He tried to sit up but couldn't.

"Flynn!" she gasped.

"You're...alive." He started coughing again and laid back down.

"Yes, Flynn, I'm alive." She smiled and squeezed his hand. "I'm here. You don't need to worry about me being safe right now, just worry about you." She leaned down and kissed him softly. "Do you think you can stay alive? Can you do it for me?"

Flynn managed a light, joking smile. "So long as that isn't the last time you kiss me, I'll stay alive as long as you want."

25- A Sign Of Loyalty

The Office, Sacramento
California, U.S.A
3:00 p.m.

Flynn

Flynn looked across the table at where Captain Vilo sat, trying to keep his face emotionless. This had been his decision. He had never thought he would stay alive to be here, but now that he was, he was ready to suffer the consequences.

It had now been two weeks since the events at Periman dock, and with the help of Blackeye and some of the best healers in the IPA, Flynn was now able to get around. Even if it was slow and still extremely painful.

They had given the pieces of the four defeated Blood Squad soldiers to the IPA for studying, and they had already given Flynn a chance to tell his story of fighting against them. Vilo had seemed very intrigued about Shark mentioning the Rift. She thought it might contain a clue as to why people were disappearing.

He now sat at the end of the table with the rest of his squad. The only person not present was Emily who, due to the decoy at the dock, was now marked as terminated by the Blood Squad. She was finally safe.

"You and the rest of your squad have violated IPA protocol," Vilo said in her cool, metallic voice. "Do you deny any of these actions?"

"No," Flynn said. "I take full responsibility for what I have done."

"Well then," she said. "The charges are simple. Flynn, because you have already been removed from the IPA, and then you continued intervening with our dealings, you have a warning. If you interfere again, we may have to formally detain you." She turned to the rest of the group. "The rest of you are removed from your service and denied any ranks you currently hold. You may go back to any homes you may have. If not, Bi will find you living accommodations. You are dismissed." The group exited the room. This kind of outcome, though disappointing, had been expected.

"Well, the days of fighting are over," Flynn said as they walked down the hallway away from the office.

Zane sighed. "I wonder what will happen to the Rizen."

"They aren't going to let us keep it," Ryan continued.

"We read about it in the IPA removal guidelines," Zane said. There was a pause in the conversation.

"You know what?" Bi said.

"What?" Zane and Ryan asked.

"I'm proud of you guys," she said. "All of you. But most of all Flynn. And not just for his skills in combat. Flynn, when you got removed from the IPA, you understood my reasoning in not standing up for you. Without me keeping the position as squad leader, we would have never had the equipment we needed to save Emily the second time." She smiled. "Of course, we wouldn't have been able to do that without you either."

Flynn shook his head. "I don't mean to get all speech-like on you guys, but there is no way I would still be alive if any of you had not been in my life. Tarff, you saved me from the juggernaut in New York. Zane, you helped me save Emily the first time by giving me information that I would have never been able to access without your help."

"Don't forget the truck," Zane said. "You still owe me a new truck."

Flynn smiled. "Ryan, you saved me and Cago that night when we almost were captured. Cago, not only have you been my friend for years before this, but even in the little time that you have been with us, you have helped me so much. And Blackeye," Flynn chuckled. "I don't even know how many times you've saved every single one of us in this group. I am a good fighter, but having multiple bullets go through me and shattering twenty-seven bones is nothing I could go up against without your help, not to mention all the times you have taken out an enemy soldier who is inches away from killing us, without ever leaving so much as a scratch on our suits."

For the first time, Blackeye seemed uncomfortable, as if she was surprised to be complimented. "Thank you, Flynn."

Flynn had heard about Blackeye speaking on the dock, but she hadn't said anything since then.

Flynn smiled. Lots of things are going to change now. He could feel it.

They reached the parking lot. Clan Vilo had been nice enough to give the group a van that was large enough to carry all of them, along with the Lamborghini that they already owned.

As they had planned before, Bi and Blackeye went to the Lamborghini. They would live together at Bi's old place, and the boys would move into the old bakery.

As they separated, no words were spoken. They all arrived at their cars and turned to the others, their fingers raised in a salute.

The salute. A sign of loyalty. They would stand up for what they knew was right. Not just for themselves, but for each other. As long as they did that, they would never be far apart.

Flynn could feel the cool grass through the back of his black T-shirt. It was now the last day of the summer, which meant school started tomorrow. So much had happened this summer, and Flynn had nearly lost his life on multiple occasions, but now all he felt was peaceful. He wasn't in a war anymore. He didn't have to fight.

Over the two weeks since separating, Ryan, Zane, Cago and Tarff had moved into the bakery with Flynn, and Blackeye had gone to live with Bi on the east side of town. The rest of the boys went to school with Flynn now, and he had finally gotten Zane his new truck. Luckily, even after what had happened last time, he had let Flynn take it to this.

Flynn looked over at Emily. The two of them were currently on a hill overlooking the city of Sacramento, gazing up at the stars. She had been naming constellations that she saw, and both of them would laugh at the stories she would tell of her and her grandfather. Her parents had been scared for Emily when they first found out what had happened, but were thankful for all that Flynn had done to try to help.

"Hey, there's Hercules," Emily said, pointing up at the sky. "My grandpa would go on for hours about Hercules." Emily continued talking about her grandparents and all the things they had done together. She shared some things that Fylnn remembered doing with his grandparents, along with things he wished he could have done but had never gotten the chance.

Over the past few weeks, she had become less self-conscious. Now that she knew the truth about Flynn, she had started to get more comfortable around him.

Tonight, she was wearing black jeans with a white T-shirt and a jean jacket on top. Her dark hair was let loose, and it flowed freely down to her shoulders. Her bright eyes reflected the stars every time she smiled.

Flynn caught himself staring at her but right now, he didn't care. She just looked so...perfect. She was the best thing that Flynn could possibly give his life to save.

She must have seen him smiling because she stopped talking and gave him a confused look. "What's so funny?"

Flynn shook his head. "Nothing, it's just a beautiful night." He reached over and grabbed a chip out of the bag next to him. They had bought tons of snacks for tonight, but had rarely eaten anything.

Emily scooted closer and leaned against him. She gazed up at the sky. The Redstone was directly above them. "You know what I wonder sometimes?" She paused. "I wonder if when someone believes in something hard enough, if it can really happen."

"So, like, placebo?" Flynn asked.

"No," Emily shook her head. "I mean like, take the Redstone for example. If someone really believed that they could save their 'Redstone', the thing they cared about most, do you really think they could?"

Flynn smiled. "Well, it sure worked for me."

She slapped him on the arm. "Stop it."

"No, I'm serious," Flynn said. "Bi couldn't describe what happened. My mind wasn't even comprehending what people were saying and yet somehow when you showed up, I came back. It wasn't even a decision I made. It was almost as if..." He sighed. "It was almost as if it was some other force that made it happen. So when you ask if I believe in it, I think I would say yes. When things that are impossible become possible, I like to have a reason for it."

She turned toward him and smiled. "You know, these things you speak of might not be as impossible as you think." She leaned her head in close to his.

Flynn hesitated. "Considering what I have been eating over the past few hours that might not be a very good-" He got cut off as she pressed her lips against his.

Flynn felt all of the pain of the past three months melt away into oblivion. The war was still going on, but right now, Flynn could feel peace. He had survived. More importantly, Emily had survived. And right now, holding her in his arms, Flynn felt like something could finally go right.

He was wrong.

Epilogue

The Outskirts, Los Angeles
California, U.S.A
9:30 p.m.
Dax

Dax held onto a pole to stabilize himself as the Lander drove along the bumpy dirt road, feeling each movement cause a cold shiver as his metal helmet brushed the top of his bald head. Dozens of soldiers were talking loudly around him, celebrating their recent victory of receiving the data chip at the base. They laughed and joked, talking about how many kills they got and making claims of buying drinks when they got back to their base.

He overlooked them with pride. This was his own personal elite squad. He was the only clan captain other than Troy to have one. Sure, they weren't as capable as him, but they made him proud nonetheless.

Dax saw a flashing light out of the corner of his eye. He reached down to his wrist and pressed a button, and his comm sparked to life. "Dax, we have a situation here in Florida." It was Troy. Clan Captain Troy. "The Ironborn warrior requests the presence of you and ten of your best soldiers. We need you to get here fast."

"How confidential is this situation?" Dax asked.

"Extremely confidential. Our researchers studied the file you sent us," Troy replied quietly. He took a deep breath. "We've found the Redstone."

Acknowledgements

I have so many people to thank when it comes to this book that I don't even know where to start. In the two years that have passed between when I wrote this at age thirteen to now, there have been so many people who have proofread my writing, given me feedback, and just genuinely made this book way better than before.

I want to thank Brandon Mull who really got me into reading and writing with his amazing books and also kindle direct publishing that made this all possible for someone as young as I am.

I also want to thank my dad and my editor Faith who were my two largest contributors to making this all a reality.

Most importantly I want to thank you, the reader, for spending your time on this book. I love this series and all of the stories it tells, and I have always been very excited to be able to share it with all of you, whoever you might be. Remember to stand up for what you believe in, no matter what.

-Kyler Wright

ABOUT THE AUTHOR

Kyler Wright is a fifteen year old author who has always loved reading and first started writing books at the age of twelve. He finished Project 1711 at the age of thirteen and is now on book three of what he plans to make into a five book series.

Kyler lives in central Utah with his two brothers, one sister, father, and pet gecko named Smawg. He has loved this story for a long time and is very excited to share it with all of you.

Flynn and our heroes will return in:

IRONBORN

CADMORE'S LIST

Made in the USA
Columbia, SC
05 July 2024

cd9d7dba-89a4-44af-ae5f-3e209a5b7f6aR01